P9-APC-737

Dear Reader,

This book has a long and checkered past. Not only has it gone through several rewrites, which included changing the setting, it also has a brand-new heroine. Trust me, Nick is much happier with this Maggie than with the last one. Although it certainly took him long enough to figure that out!

Yes, Nick is as stubborn as the day is long, but he'll do anything to protect those he loves, even if it means dying. He needed a woman strong enough to challenge him, and I think Maggie does that and more. I hope you agree!

Next up, I'm writing a trilogy set on the fictitious and quaint, but not so quiet Mirabelle Island. Keep an eye out for those books in 2009. While you're waiting, check out my Harlequin NASCAR series titles. You don't have to be crazy for racing to love these romances.

Peace and happiness,

Helen Brenna

FINDING MR. RIGHT
Helen Brenna

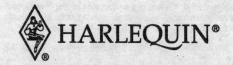

TORONTO • NEW YORK • LONDON
AMSTERDAM • PARIS • SYDNEY • HAMBURG
STOCKHOLM • ATHENS • TOKYO • MILAN • MADRID
PRAGUE • WARSAW • BUDAPEST • AUCKLAND

ISBN-13: 978-0-373-71519-0
ISBN-10:   0-373-71519-6

FINDING MR. RIGHT

ABOUT THE AUTHOR

Helen Brenna grew up the seventh of eight children in central Minnesota. Although as a child she never dreamed of writing stories, she was a voracious reader, cutting her teeth on all the Harlequin books she could get her hands on.

With a B.S. in accounting, she started career life as a CPA and thought she'd end career life as an old CPA, but the decision to stay home with her kids made all things possible. Helen's books have been nominated for Romance Writers of America's prestigious RITA® Awards and for a Reviewer's Choice award from *Romantic Times BOOKreviews*.

She continues to write away, living in Minnesota with her husband, two children, two dogs and three surly (who can blame them?) cats. She would love to hear from you. E-mail her at helenbrenna@comcast.net or send mail to P.O. Box 24107, Minneapolis, Minnesota 55424.

Bloggers can chat with Helen and several other authors at ridingwiththetopdown.blogspot.com, or you can visit her Web site at www.helenbrenna.com.

Books by Helen Brenna

HARLEQUIN SUPERROMANCE
1403—TREASURE
1425—DAD FOR LIFE

For
Grandpa Wilbur and Grandma Lillian
married 76 years
That's what I call a romance!

Acknowledgments:

A long time ago Nick Bluhm bent my ear
about the satellite telephone industry.
His invaluable input helped in creating the
first incarnation of this story and taught me
the value of research. Appreciate it, Nick.

Thanks also to Mary Cosgrove for helping me
transform Maggie from computer neophyte into
hacker extraordinaire. So glad we met at the
playground all those years ago and have kept in
touch. Any and all errors are mine.

Special thanks to
Tina Wexler and Johanna Raisanen
for helping make this book the best it could be.
I sleep better knowing you two have my back.

And love to my Princesses: Fiona, Buttercup,
Aurora, Xena, Leia, Frostine, Jasmine,
Quay of the Milky Way and Honorary Sarah.
You guys rock my tiara!
Princess Wannabe

PROLOGUE

Athens, Greece

"'TODAY IS A GOOD DAY TO DIE.'" Resignation filled Yanni Kythos's deep voice.

"That's all the note said?" Nick Ballos crossed his arms and paced beside his black BMW.

"That's it."

"Do the police have any leads?"

"They think some new terrorist group is targeting the Kythos empire. Possibly planning a kidnapping." Yanni sighed and shook his head. "This...so soon after my father's death."

"Your family's vulnerable."

"Why target me?" He threw his hands wide. "It's common knowledge my father disinherited me months before his death. The tabloids had a field day with *Patera*'s will."

"Your mother would still pay a ransom."

"Stephano wouldn't let her." At the mention of his brother, Yanni grew more agitated. "You saw him. At our father's funeral. After all these years, he still wouldn't talk to me." A hot, dry breeze brought the heady scent of olive trees in bloom across the courtyard. "He blames me for *Patera*'s death. I could see it in his eyes."

That's not all Nick had seen in Stephano's eyes, but he wasn't about to reopen old wounds. Yanni had enough on his plate. "Let me go to Piraeus," he offered. "I can read the contracts in the car."

"This is my deal. My responsibility."

"Yanni—"

"I'll be back tonight." He held out his hand, dismissing the subject. "And Costas will be coming."

"A bodyguard helps, but you're still the easiest mark in your family." Nick eyed the armed guards, one near the gate and two flanking each end of the cobblestone courtyard. "Your family's compound probably has ten times the security."

"I'm not worried for me." Yanni's accent grew thick as he focused his gaze a short distance away. Kyrena, Yanni's wife, sat in the grass and played with their young son, Nestor, under the shade of an ancient cypress, while Christine, their three-month-old daughter, lay cradled in her lap. His frown deepened. "If anything happened to them…"

"On my life." Nick held a hand over his heart. "Kyrena and the children will be safe. And you'll make it through this. You always do, right?"

As he watched the play of emotion on Yanni's face, Nick couldn't help but wonder how his friend had managed to build such a full life, balancing love with the needs of a start-up business and a young family. It all seemed too complicated. Work, a few good friends, and an occasional, casual romance was all Nick had ever wanted, all he'd ever needed.

Kyrena glanced up and yelled, "Look at you two. So serious."

"You haven't told her, have you?"

"No." Yanni shook his head. "Don't you dare worry her."

Holding the sleepy baby in her arms, she took Nestor by the hand and walked toward them. Her straight black hair fell forward and a golden heart pendant slipped from under her blouse, swinging back and forth. "You haven't seen each other for months," she said. "You should be enjoying this beautiful morning. Isn't that right, Nestor?"

The boy nodded, his brown eyes big and round.

"Of course we should." Yanni scooped him up, and Kyrena tucked herself under Yanni's arm. "You and I and Kyrena." Yanni slapped Nick on the shoulder. "Like old times."

"Not quite." Nick laughed and ruffled the hair on each child's head.

But it wasn't just marriage and children that had altered things between them. Most of those old times had included Stephano. They'd been the four musketeers until hormones had started flowing. Kyrena had grown into a beautiful young woman and Nick had been forced to choose between the two brothers. The decision had been easy. Although his young family had kept Yanni in Greece and the business had taken Nick to the U.S., Nick and Yanni's friendship had not only never faltered, it had grown stronger.

Yanni fingered the heart pendant around Kyrena's neck. "You've always had my heart."

"And you mine."

Nick laughed. "Don't you two ever give it a rest?"

"Never," Yanni said. "Some day it'll hit you, Nick. Then I'll be the one laughing."

They all glanced up as a car stopped at the security

gate, signaling the arrival of Yanni's new assistant who would be attending the meeting with him in Piraeus. At Yanni's signal, the guard opened the gate and the green Audi sedan pulled into the courtyard.

"*Parakalo*, Dimitri, come," Yanni yelled as their newest employee crossed the courtyard. "This is Dimitri Gavras. My partner, Nick Ballos."

The man wore a heavy gold chain around his neck. It was gaudy and pretentious, and Nick immediately disliked him. "*Kaleemera*, Dimitri." He shook the man's hand.

Gavras nodded politely, but said nothing, as if words were too much effort. Pretentious *and* arrogant. Knowing Yanni, he'd hired the man intending on re-forming the poor bastard.

"We must be off." Yanni bent to give Kyrena a long and slow kiss goodbye. "And you, Nestor. *Andeeo*, sweet child." Yanni smacked a wet one on his son's cheek. "I'll be home in time to read tonight." He set the boy down and kissed baby Christine's forehead, then he waved to Nick. "*Andeeo,* brother. Plan a special dinner to celebrate this new contract."

Nick nodded. "Be careful."

Yanni and Gavras walked across the wide driveway. Costas, the bodyguard traveling with Yanni, climbed behind the wheel of the silver Mercedes and Yanni took the backseat. Gavras set his briefcase inside the car. "I forgot my sunglasses," he said and headed back toward his own car while motioning for the security guard to open the front gate.

Glaring sunlight reflected off Gavras's gold chain, and something, to Nick, seemed off. What was Gavras about? And why was he now practically run—

"Yanni!" Nick shot forward. "Out of the car!"

Yanni glanced back. And the Mercedes exploded.

Nick flew through the air and slammed into the pavement on the other side of the drive. Spears of broken glass and jagged metal struck him in the face and chest. On some distant plane of reality, he felt burning heat and searing pain, saw blood on his hands and on the paving stones and knew it to be his own, but it didn't seem to matter. There was something…someone…

Then Kyrena screamed. She ran toward the burning car with Chrissy in her arms and Nestor toddling after.

"No! Kyrena!" Dragging himself to his feet, Nick struggled to reach her. He tackled her and covered her and the two children with his own body right before the flames penetrated the Mercedes' fuel tank.

As the secondary explosion shook the ground, the security guards reacted. Too late, gunshots pinged ineffectively through the air as the green Audi sped through the open gate and out of sight.

Disoriented, Nick lifted his head. A blaze devoured Yanni's Mercedes. "No!" he yelled as everything came back to him. It couldn't be. Yanni couldn't be dead. His mind rejected the notion even as the acrid smell of charred leather singed his nostrils, even as thick plumes of black smoke rose into the clear blue Athens sky.

Only one thought occupied his mind before unconsciousness claimed him. He would find Dimitri Gavras and kill him. Nick would kill him, or die trying.

CHAPTER ONE

"GOTCHA!" Maggie Dillon grinned as the United States's government seal blossomed on her computer screen. It'd taken some time, but she'd finally hacked into the FBI's main database.

Wait a minute. Her initial excitement fading, she leaned back in her chair. The auxiliary security software her company had designed for the FBI obviously hadn't done its job. "Dang it." She fingered down the first of several meticulously arranged stacks of files, pulled out her work-in-progress notebook, and jotted down a few notes for her programming team. That was one back door that needed closing pronto.

"This will make your day." Shannon, Maggie's younger sister and second-in-command breezed into Maggie's office sounding mighty pleased with herself. "I finally found him. The perfect man."

"You sure this time?"

"Positive." Shannon held out a thick manila folder. "On second thought," she said, pulling the file back, "maybe I'll keep him for myself."

"Gimme that already!" Maggie snatched the papers.

She'd spent the last two months looking for a guy with the right combination of business experience and knowledge of Greek customs to run point for her in negotiations with Greece's national defense department. If Shannon and the talent scout they'd hired had finally found the right man, Maggie couldn't afford to waste a single precious minute.

"You used to be fun," Shannon said, pouting. "What happened to you?"

Life had happened.

There was nothing like being solely responsible for two younger sisters to yank a person onto the straight and narrow. And nothing like the baby sister's looming college tuition to make business expansion a necessity. Hell, she'd barely recovered from Shannon's stint at Georgetown.

Maggie flicked at the edges of the bulging file. "Looks like Dawkins went overboard here."

"Probably had something to do with you chewing his butt over the last prospect turning out to be a convicted felon."

"Did you read all this?"

"Every juicy tidbit."

Maggie cleared a space on her desktop, laid the file down and flipped through the papers, intending to read only the most pertinent business information. She glanced down at what was probably a company head shot clipped to the outside jacket of the file. Impeccable black suit. Short dark hair. Impressive wasn't the only adjective Maggie would've used to describe this guy. That faded scar angling down his right cheekbone gave him a serious, almost lethal appearance.

Damn! It riled her that she actually needed a *man* for anything, let alone one as virile-looking as this. Call her sexist, but she did not want to be working in the same office with this obvious a distraction. "Shred this folder." She pushed away the paperwork and grabbed one of the many three-dimensional puzzles sitting on her desk. "What does Dawkins think I'm looking for? A mercenary playing *GQ* model?"

"Snagged your line, didn't he?" Shannon asked, one eyebrow arched.

"Rich and sexy?" She rotated a section of the puzzle, aligning the set of numbers. "Your type, not mine."

Shannon laughed. "You've got more strike-outs than D.C. has monuments. Maybe it's time you try someone different."

"It's been a tough day." Maggie tossed the cube back onto her desk and rubbed her screen-tired eyes. "I'll ignore that."

"Suit yourself." Shannon shrugged. "His father was only the American ambassador to Greece, so our man grew up there. Probably has all the right connections, but what do I know?"

Maggie considered the folder again. She pinched two dead leaves off the African violet inhabiting one corner of her desk before curiosity finally won out and she pulled the file back. "What's his name?"

"Nicholas Ballos."

The sound of his name immediately conjured images of sultry Mediterranean nights and delightful ocean breezes. "He's American?"

"Yep. His father emigrated from Greece when he was ten. His mother's a native Californian." Shannon headed for the door. "I'll go get us something to drink."

Doing her best to ignore the irrelevant personal details, Maggie scanned the paperwork. Not only had Ballos grown up in Greece, but he'd also owned a successful international shipping company based out of

Baltimore, proving he had good business sense. When Shannon returned a few minutes later, Maggie glanced at her. "This guy's the real thing."

Shannon winked, setting two cans of diet soda between them. "I told you."

"There's only one problem." Maggie tapped the desktop. "He's so impressive, he has no reason to go for what we can offer." She gazed out her window, through the hanging mass of ivy and purple passion vine, at the midsummer heat and humidity rising in waves off the street below. Their offices might sit at a high point in the Adams-Morgan district, but there was nothing impressive about them.

On the block directly across from their mostly—restored brownstone, the neon light advertising psychic readings was missing the *P*, the mom-and-pop Mexican restaurant did barely enough business to keep its doors open, and the bookstore on the corner had a going out of business sign in its window. Not a thriving neighborhood by any means.

Still, the property came cheap, offered a relatively central location, and the top-floor apartment space was large enough to accommodate Maggie, Shannon—once upon a time—and their younger sister, Kate. Not to mention the building management had allowed Maggie to build a small greenhouse on part of the large roof area opening off her bedroom. It might be an empty greenhouse, at the moment, but it was there all the same, waiting for the day when Maggie could make time for plants outside of the pots in her office.

"Why should he punch a clock for us?" Maggie mused.

"He has lots of time on his hands. Why not?"

"Because he recently sold his company for a helluva

lot of money. Which probably means he'll be retiring and sailing around the world, or whatever else it is that filthy rich people do."

Shannon perched on the edge of Maggie's desk. "He's only in his early thirties. And, from all accounts, definitely not the type to play away the rest of his life."

"Isn't it odd he hasn't been anywhere near Greece, let alone the Mediterranean, for years?"

"He's been busy running his company."

"That originally did a great deal of shipping out of Greece. Presumably, he'd have friends there, family to visit." Maggie tapped the papers in the file. "Maybe he doesn't want to go back. Maybe he hated it there. Maybe—"

"Where's the harm in presenting your case?"

Maggie sighed. "How do we convince him to meet with me?" Shannon's cat-got-the-canary smile told her that the issue had already been addressed. She chuckled. "Who knows someone who knows someone who knows him?"

"His parents were longtime family friends of Senator Howard Stiles."

"And?"

"I roomed with the Senator's niece freshman year." Shannon smirked. "Uncle Howie made a call, and our Mr. Right will be here in…" Shannon said, looking down at her watch. "Ten minut—"

"Your *Mr. Right*'s here now."

Maggie spun her chair toward the sound of the man's voice. *Oh, boy.* That company head shot had nothing on the actual sight of Nicholas Ballos. He leaned against the door frame, nearly filling the open space. In black dress pants and a long-sleeved white shirt, he looked crisp, cool. This, after coming in from a muggy, one-hundred-and-two-degrees-in-the-shade July day. His hair was longer than in the picture and a heavy strand strayed low on his brow. If not for the scar on his cheek, more prevalent in person than in his picture, he may have seemed almost approachable.

She set his paperwork in a side desk drawer as inconspicuously as possible. Something told her this man wouldn't take kindly to having his life summarized in a file.

"Hello, Mr. Right." Shannon swaggered toward him. "I'm Shannon Dillon."

"Ms. Dillon," he said. "Apparently, you pulled the strings to get me here."

"I doubt mere strings would've done the trick." Grinning, Shannon turned on her natural charm. "Curiosity maybe?"

He tilted his head. "Got me there."

Oh, please! Maggie barely kept herself from rolling her eyes. She stood, pasting a smile on her face. "Hello, Nicholas." She'd be damned if she was going to call him mister, let alone Mr. Right. "I'm Shannon's sister, Maggie Dillon." She shook his hand, and, the moment they touched, the playful curve at the corner of his lips disappeared.

"Call me Nick." He studied her, deliberately, even had balls enough to give her hand a slight twist in order to get a better look at the tattoo on the inside of her wrist.

Yeah, you got it. A tattoo. Wanna see my piercings, rich boy? She tucked her hair behind her ears, displaying an impressive row of studs, hoops and ear cuffs. *Bite me, Mr. Right.*

As usual, whenever the upper-crusty acquaintances

Shannon had made at Georgetown compared the two sisters, Maggie's insecurities flared and her armor deployed. She didn't have a college degree backing her play, let alone a high school diploma. Her GED and this business were the only things between her and minimum wage. And at a scrappy five-foot-two with unruly auburn hair, she'd never measured up to Shannon's natural elegance. Not that Maggie normally tried to, but, at this moment, she wouldn't have minded appearing refined and irresistibly attractive.

For once.

Difficult to do wearing a T-shirt imprinted with the saying, *One woman, two digits, who needs a man?*

Putting on what she hoped was a natural smile, Maggie directed him to the other side of her office, to what her programmers called the chitchat pit while Shannon grabbed a pad of paper and sat down to take notes. Instead of a conference table, Maggie had arranged a sofa and several chairs around a large square coffee table, creating an informal meeting area.

"Thanks for agreeing to meet on such short notice." Maggie sat in one of the chairs and motioned him across from her. "I don't want to waste your time, so I'll get right to the point." As he leaned back, his long legs kicked out in front of him, a tuft of midnight-black hair eased over the top button of his shirt. Without thinking, she blurted out, "I need a man. It's as simple as that."

Other than his eyes narrowing slightly, he didn't move. "I'm sure, Maggie, you deserve nothing less."

Arrogant. Too good-looking. And not her type. Still, her fingers itched to touch the curious scar on his cheek, to undo a few more buttons on that starched shirt.

She took a deep breath and exhaled slowly. "Let me

back up. My company, Universal Security, has recently developed and patented a software product that provides auxiliary security for computer systems. What I should have said is *Universal Security* needs a man," she said, "with your background to market the software."

"My background?" he said, shaking his head. "Wrong man. I don't know anything about computers, software or security."

"I have a technical staff," she explained. "What I need is someone who can handle themselves around high-level government officials and negotiate contracts. You ran your own company for years. That kind of experience is invaluable."

Ballos swung his arm around the back of his chair and gazed around the room, appearing to digest the information. If he was half as arrogant and judgmental as he looked, he wasn't going to think much of her company. She was profitable but small with only two offices, hers and Shannon's. Her programmers, nothing more than a group of hackers, worked from their respective homes.

She and Shannon might have up-to-the-minute computer systems and large offices but their furniture was a mish-mash of pieces Maggie and Shannon had found at estate and garage sales. Office casual? Try jeans and T-shirts. Sometimes shorts. Their central air had been known to crash like an overloaded hard drive, especially on days as hot as today.

"You want *me* to work for *you*?" he finally said.

See? "My company may not initially be able to offer you much, but we're growing. We have tremendous potential."

"I'm sure you do." He stood and headed for the door. "The answer's no."

Maggie scrambled. Kate's college tuition was walking out the door. "I guess you're not the man I thought you were if you can leave without hearing me out."

He turned. "While you personally might need a man, Maggie, I doubt your company does. You seem more than capable of negotiating your own contracts."

"Not in Greece," she returned softly and watched his reaction. "And not with their current Minister of Public Order."

Surprise registered in his eyes and something else— pain or fear, she couldn't tell which—before he strode past her to stop in front of one of three old-fashioned paned windows.

After following him behind her desk, she studied his profile. Several strands of gray at his temples had become more visible with the sun streaming through the glass, but a wall had been raised around him. Dress him in the appropriate uniform and with that stoic expression he'd easily pass for a guard at Buckingham Palace.

"The Minister of Public Order has been giving me the brush off for months," she said. "You negotiate the contracts. In return, you take a commission. You'll walk away with an easy $50,000—"

"I don't need the money." His voice was a monotone, emotionless.

"Look at the challenge, then."

"Doesn't sound like much of one to me. A dose of testosterone, and you've got it bagged."

"That's not true. There are several companies that have put in bids. Your expertise in Greek customs might sway the ultimate decision our way. I realize you haven't been there for some time, but having grown up in Greece should more than make up for that."

He turned suddenly and frowned at her. "You know an awful lot about me."

Maggie lifted her chin defensively. "My company wouldn't be where it is today if I didn't do my research."

She was close enough to see his pulse beating at his neck, to watch his scar pale against his darkening skin. She'd been right. He was lethal. Volatile. Probably not just a rich snob. She took a step back and felt for the edge of her desk.

"Your company. It means a lot to you, doesn't it?" He moved toward her.

"I won't let this contract slip through my fingers without a damned good fight, if that's what you mean."

"I think you know what I mean."

He had to be trying to intimidate her. He certainly couldn't find her attractive. His type of woman would have diamonds dripping off her earlobes, designer rags, manicured hands. Maggie's nails were clipped short, her jeans were old and holey, which only by coincidence happened to be fashionable, and her flip-flops were definitely not Jimmy Choo.

"Look," she said, "if you don't want to do this, I'll find someone else."

"I almost believe you're holding the cards, Maggie." He smiled then, a slick, condescending number that had Maggie folding her arms and glaring at him. "Will you be going to Athens?" he asked. "Working with their government systems?"

"Eventually. If we get the contract, I'll be going over there with a team of programmers. But you wouldn't need to trav—"

"I want in on all of it."

"You have no systems experience."

"Train me."

"Why?"

"Those are my conditions. You want me in or out?"

She didn't have a choice. Greece's Minister of Public Order was closing the bidding process next week. "In."

"Good." A slow smile traveled from his lips to his eyes. "I'll have my attorney draft the agreements, and I'll see you Monday morning."

As he walked out of the room, Maggie felt no sense of victory. His closeness, the scent of him—fresh air and male heat—left her with the sickening feeling that he'd never really work for her. He'd only let her believe it.

"Of all the—" She strode to the doorway. "There's a retirement party at General Walker's estate in Alexandria tomorrow night," she called out to him as he stepped into the elevator. "Be there."

The door slid closed before she could hear his response. With a frustrated sigh, she walked back into the room, her head bowed in concentration.

"He went for it," Shannon said from her position in the chitchat pit.

Startled, Maggie looked behind her to find Shannon's face lit with a mischievous smile. "Wow. I forgot you were in the room."

"Somehow that doesn't surprise me." Shannon stood up. "That was easier than I'd expect."

"Maybe a little too easy," Maggie mused.

"If I were to guess, I'd say he'll be looking for a bonus from you and I don't think it'll involve cash, check or charge."

Maggie dropped into the chair behind her desk. "He'll be of no interest to me once the contracts are signed."

"Come on, Maggie. Watching the two of you together was like watching…foreplay."

"That's his game." Maggie laughed. "He uses sex to intimidate women."

"I don't think so." Shannon shook her head. "I've got a good feeling about Nick Ballos."

Maggie didn't. She could barely keep herself from fidgeting with the pencil lying on top of her desk. Sure, he was attractive, but there was something unsettling about him. She opened the drawer and flipped through the talent scout's file.

"What are you looking for?" Shannon rounded the desk.

There it was. Maggie stared at the harmless tidbit of personal information. "I knew it," she whispered. Her morals might be a little worse for wear, but she had them all the same.

"What?" Shannon asked.

"He's married." Maggie closed the file and pushed it away. "Nick Ballos is married. With two kids."

CHAPTER TWO

OLD MONEY.

The sprawling structure of stone and slate screamed of generations of wealth and power. The Walker estate was in all its glory tonight, bright lights shining through every window, the sound of laughter spilling out the doors, and the melodious strains of a string quartet drifting through the warm night air.

A party. Whoop-de-do.

This was the last place Nick wanted to be, but he couldn't pass up the chance that Giannis Ramos, Greece's Minister of Public Order and an old friend of Nick's father, might be here tonight. All Nick had to do was convince him that Nick's reason for returning to Greece was legitimate. That shouldn't be too hard given his new job.

Nick tossed his car keys to a valet and ascended the wide marble steps. Once inside the foyer, he adjusted to the brilliance of twinkling chandeliers before heading to the ballroom through a throng of guests. On his way, he lifted a glass of champagne from a passing waiter's tray and perused the crowd. Congressmen, ambassadors, heads of state. Maggie certainly knew how to pick 'em. Everyone who was anyone in foreign relations was at General Walker's retirement party.

Hadn't he expected as much? With connections to a U.S. Senator, Maggie Dillon could hardly have been involved in anything less grand. She might look the part of an anything-goes hacker with her low-budget office décor, smart-aleck T-shirt, and messy curls, but his new boss was as shrewd a woman as they come. One look in her amber eyes had confirmed there wasn't a soft spot or smooth edge on the woman. She didn't give a damn about anything except achieving her own objectives. Fine by him. As long as she didn't interfere with his plans, he wouldn't interfere with hers.

The only problem was that tough, only-came-up-to-his-chin Maggie stirred in Nick more than thoughts of business. Tattoos? Ear cuffs? Since when had flip-flops turned him on? He put it down to having gone too long without a woman.

Good thing he was finally, after more than three years, in a position to rectify that situation. That is, after he finished his business in Greece. And if he came back alive.

A hand clamped down on his shoulder, and years of martial arts training kicked in. He spun around.

"Whoa! Down boy." Craig Stanton's hands flew up in mock surrender. "Damn, you take that karate stuff way too seriously."

"Sorry." Nick relaxed. For years, he'd been preparing himself for his eventual return to Greece, and the fact that it was almost at hand had him on full alert.

"You're the last person I expected to see here tonight." Craig chuckled. "I thought you hated these things."

"I do." For as long as Nick could remember he'd felt awkward in social settings. He downed half his glass and scanned the crowd over the rim of the delicate flute. A roomful of people had a way of setting him on edge.

"Hello, Stanton." A beautiful brunette in a flashy red dress sidled up to Craig. "Who's your friend?"

"Nick, this is Marsha, a senior attorney at my firm."

"Hello, Nick." Her voice was slow, thick, making her intentions clear.

Nick glanced away. While eager was always good, foaming at the mouth had never done much for him. "Not interested."

She laughed. "Straight up. I can appreciate that. See you later, Craig."

As she moved on to her next potential victim, Craig shook his head. "Do you *ever* intend on learning a few social graces?"

"What would be the point?" Nick shook his head. "By the way, where the hell were you the other night? We had a basketball court reserved for nine-thirty."

"I was, ah…preoccupied," Craig mumbled, rubbing his cleanly shaven chin.

Nick followed Craig's gaze. "With Long Legs in the pink dress? That is if you can call it a dress. If that thing was any shorter it could double as a scarf."

"What can I say? A leg man until I die." Craig shrugged, then turned his full attention on Nick. "The last payment from Hamilton Shipping was wired into your account yesterday. Your company is officially sold."

"Thanks for smoothing things out."

"Doing my job."

"And then some." Nick nodded in the direction of the sexy blonde in the frilly pink dress. "You should take Long Legs off for some tropical R and R."

"We're going island hopping in the Caribbean in a few weeks. What about you? You've got more than the sale of your company to celebrate."

Nick rubbed his left hand. The absence of the ring still felt strange.

"Man," Craig said, shaking his head. "I can't believe you never once saw another woman, all those years."

"A vow is a vow."

"It wasn't re—"

"Yes, it was," Nick quickly interrupted. "In every way except one."

"I could make some introductions." Craig glanced around. "Marsha obviously wasn't your type—"

"Tonight's business. I'm looking for my new boss."

Craig nearly choked on his champagne. "Boss?"

Nick nodded while watching the crowd for a distinctive red head. "An opportunity presented itself, and I jumped on it."

"Must have been some deal for you to take a backseat."

"I had my reasons."

Silent for a moment, Craig studied him. "This is about Yanni, isn't it?"

Though Craig had been a good friend as well as Nick's main legal counsel for many years, he still didn't, probably couldn't, understand. But for someone like Nick, who was, admittedly, as social as a rock, losing Yanni, friend, business partner, all rolled into one, had been like losing a lung.

"You can't be thinking of going back to Greece."

"Not thinking. Doing."

The private investigators he'd hired through the years hadn't discovered one shred of useful evidence concerning Yanni's murder, let alone located Dimitri Gavras. It hadn't helped that the Greek government had classified all of Yanni's information, considering the bombing a terrorist act and therefore a matter of national security. Nick had the distinct impression they were keeping something under wraps, and this job with Maggie was his ticket into Yanni's classified files.

"If Stephano catches you back in Greece…he's not going to be happy."

"That's his problem." Kyrena and the children were safe now. That's all that mattered.

Craig shook his head. "God, I envy you sometimes. Everything is black and white, isn't it?"

Nick shrugged. "I'm hungry, I eat. I'm tired, I sleep." There was no such thing as a gray area.

"Going back won't change anything."

"No," Nick agreed, finishing off the last of his champagne. It would, though, pay a long overdue debt. He been forced to wait several years before making a move. If that wasn't long enough for the Greek government to find Gavras, it was time for someone else to take a shot.

He set the empty flute on a waiter's tray, grabbed another one, and a flash of unmistakable red hair flickered at the edge of his vision. That couldn't be her. He looked again. It was. Maggie Dillon, talking and laughing with a large group not twenty feet away.

To say she cleaned up nicely would have been a gross understatement. The woman had completely transformed. She'd nearly tamed her wild curls by loosely sweeping them upward into some kind of clip, making it clear she'd traded in her line of studs and ear cuffs for dangling black pearls. A wide band of beads covered the tattoo on the inside of her wrist. Outfitted in a simple black column dress with a high neckline and cap sleeves, she looked almost modest—that is, until she started walking.

That's when a slit in her dress, running from her

ankle clear to her hip, became apparent. Rather than hanging blatantly open, intermittent strands of tiny black beads connected the fabric. In one moment, Nick was treated to a clear look at her ankle or knee, in another, a glimpse of shapely thigh. He wasn't sure he liked the mystery of it all. Then again, maybe he liked it too much.

"Speaking of bosses," Nick said clearing his head, "that's her. Over there."

"Ah, hell," Craig muttered. "Not the blonde in blue sequins."

Nick hadn't even noticed that woman. "You know Shannon Dillon?"

"Unfortunately. If you've signed on with her, you'd better watch your back, your wallet and your heart."

Birds of a feather, Nick reminded himself as Maggie caught sight of him. "Actually, it's the woman in black heading this way."

"Shannon's sister. My firm does some legal work for them now and then."

"Hey, Craig." Maggie squeezed through the crowd. "Glad to see you made it tonight, Nick."

"The way you phrased the invitation," he returned softly, "didn't exactly leave many options."

"It's been a long time, Maggie," Craig said. "Good to see you again."

"What are you doing here?" She swatted Craig's shoulder. "I thought you weren't the slightest bit interested in foreign affairs."

"I've been told there were clients to be had in these parts." Craig held his arms out to his sides. "So here I am."

"And, my, aren't we lucky?" Shannon's deep voice rolled toward them.

Though Craig looked as if he'd reined his temper in tight enough to choke himself, Shannon appeared unfazed.

"We haven't seen much of you," Maggie said, "since you turned our workload over to another associate at your firm."

"There was a slight conflict of interest." He looked past her toward Shannon.

"Oh, please!" Shannon raised an eyebrow. "We're supposed to believe you've actually acquired some ethical standards?"

Craig returned his attention to Maggie. "As always, Maggie, you're simply stunning tonight. Why did you have to spoil the look by bringing along the blonde viper?"

Drinks *and* a show. Nick swallowed back a laugh with a gulp of champagne.

"I see you're full of your usual brilliant compliments this evening."

"What can I say? You inspire me."

"That reminds me." Shannon's voice dripped with sickening sweetness. "We saw your newest conquest on the way in. You'd better run along and tend to her before someone mistakes her for a talking Barbie doll and takes her home for the kiddies to play with. On second thought," she said, pausing in mock concentration, "talking would imply she had a brain, and we know that's not very like—"

"Oh, stop it," Maggie interrupted and Nick couldn't keep the chuckle from rumbling out. "You two haven't seen each other for months. The least you could do is be civil."

"Craig and I, civil?" Shannon snorted softly. "The day I pitch a tent on the Mall and roast marshmallows over a roaring fire." She walked away.

"Don't pay any attention to her," Maggie offered.

"Easier said than done." Craig laughed. "Sorry I can't stay and catch up, Mags, but I suddenly need something stronger than champagne. Excuse me."

Maggie shook her head. "Those two need a referee."

More like a king-sized bed, if you asked Nick.

With the entertainment gone, he became aware of Maggie standing too close. A light, powdery smell drifted upward from her hair, in refreshing counterpoint to the heavy perfumes pushing in around them. "Who did you want me to meet?" he said, stepping back.

"Not into the party?" She smirked.

The black pearls dangling from her earlobes swung back and forth, and Nick noticed several curls had fallen from her clip. It was all he could do to keep from twirling his finger around a chunk and drawing her near.

"I would have guessed this was your crowd."

"Hardly." Kiss her neck, that's what he wanted to do.

Nearby, a woman in a white halter dress was sizing him up. Before she could make a move toward him, Nick turned his back on her and tucked a hand under Maggie's arm, drawing her away. "Let's get our business done, so I can get out of here."

"That was quite a brush-off," she said, an edge to her voice. "Did you know the woman in white?"

"No, and I don't care to. Who're we looking for?"

"Greece's Minister of Public Order. He's in town for this party."

Good. She *was* expecting Giannis tonight.

"Minister Ramos won't return my calls," she explained. "Maybe you'll have better luck."

No surprise there. Giannis always had been old school. They both glanced around, and Maggie finally nodded toward a set of French doors opening to the verandah. "There he is. Heading outside."

"Let's go." He put his hand at the small of her back and led her through the crowd.

"Did you read through that paperwork I sent you along with the invitation to this party?"

"I won't have any problems carrying myself in a conversation, if that's what you're worried about."

"He's over there." Her gaze rested on a portly man with streaks of gray flashing through his black hair.

The man turned toward the doors bringing his face into clear view. It *was* Giannis. *Piece of cake.* "Follow my lead." Before Maggie could object, Nick stepped around her. "*Kalispera*, Minister. One moment of your time, *parakalo*."

Giannis glanced over at them. "Nicholas!" He clasped Nick's hand between both of his and kissed him on each cheek. "I haven't seen you since…" The minister's eyes closed briefly as a solemn expression overtook his pudgy features. "Well, it's been a long time." He regarded Nick for a moment, then rested his hand against his heart. "I just spoke with your father. He and your mother seem content in California."

"They're enjoying retirement." Nick turned to his side. "Maggie, this is Giannis Ramos, an old friend of my family's. Giannis, this is Maggie Dillon."

"Miss Dillon." The minister dipped his head and shook her hand.

"It's a pleasure to meet you, Minister Ramos."

Giannis continued holding her hand. "I believe I've had a few voice mails from you."

"I'm afraid so."

Chuckling, he dropped her hand. "I apologize. I've

been traveling quite a bit these days and haven't been able to return all my calls."

"I would have called you myself," Nick said. "But Maggie jumped the gun. She's my assistant in a new business I'm pursuing."

Maggie glowered at Nick over the minister's lowered head, and he held his breath, hoping she wouldn't blow this. As long as he got the results she was looking for, what difference did it make?

"I got involved in the security software business quite recently," Nick continued, "and I understand your government is looking for bids to upgrade your security."

"That's correct."

Maggie took a step forward, as if she might speak. Nick touched her arm, holding her back, and said, "Please give me the honor, Giannis, of considering my proposal."

Giannis narrowed his eyes. "You realize that if you win the bid, you'd be required to return to Athens?"

"Of course," Nick said. "But I believe the past should stay there," he finished in Greek, hoping Giannis would follow his lead. The less Maggie knew the better.

"If only Stephano Kythos felt the same way," Giannis whispered back, also in Greek.

"You know those child endangerment charges against Kyrena were fabricated."

"Yes." Gianni nodded. "But the case has never been closed. Stephano may try to bring charges against you for taking Kyrena and the children out of the country."

"So be it."

"One would've hoped marriage would temper him."

"I'm not counting on it." From what Nick had heard, Mother Kythos had been pestering Stephano for grandchildren. The recent union between her son and a young heiress named Talia probably had more to do with gene pools and political positioning than emotion.

Giannis sighed. "All right, then, send your bid to my office at the Greek Embassy." He finished their discussion in English. "After I have a chance to review it, we can schedule a meeting to discuss your proposal."

"I appreciate this."

Again, the minister grasped Nick's hand between both of his. "We'll visit next week. For now, I must go. General Walker is looking for me. *Adio*, Nicholas." He nodded at Maggie. "Miss Dillon."

"Minister Ramos." She smiled.

"*Adio*, Giannis."

After Giannis was well out of earshot Maggie turned to him. "So now I'm an *assistant*. Nice to be demoted within my own company."

"You got what you wanted, Maggie."

"You could have told him we were associates."

"I could have." He cocked his head to one side. "And in the process lost some respect. He needed to believe I'm more than your employee."

As the warm summer night closed in around them, vulnerability flashed in her eyes. She spun away, her frustration palpable. God help him, but he understood. Once again, his reaction to this paradox of a woman was primal and swift. Maybe he wouldn't be waiting until he returned from Greece to deal with this attraction.

"Look." He drew her toward the edge of the verandah and lowered his voice. "Isn't this what you needed me for?"

"I know why I hired you," she whispered. "The real question is why did you take the job."

CHAPTER THREE

"TELL ME YOU NOTICED the way he looked at you," Shannon said, sipping a Monday morning latte.

Maggie had thought of little else since Saturday night. Nick Ballos had not only undressed her with his eyes at the Walker party, he'd done so with a distinctly unapologetic air. Even the memory of the heat in his eyes, as much as she hated to admit it, made her skin sizzle with a crazy kind of expectation.

"The other women at that party could've been buck naked for all he knew." Shannon tore off a hunk of flaky croissant and popped it in her mouth. "The only woman Nick Ballos noticed was you."

"He's married. Remember?" Maggie leaned back on the chaise lounge in her greenhouse and stared over the top of the *Washington Post*.

"So what?" Shannon shrugged.

Obviously, Maggie had been rubbing off on her sister. Too much. It was so damned hard trying to be a good role model, when, well, you weren't.

"That's not the same as saying he uses a Mac, I use a PC. This is wife and two kids, 'til death do us part." Maggie went back to her newspaper, but it was hard concentrating after being reminded of what Nick Ballos had looked like in a tux. "Besides, even if he wasn't taken, I'd want nothing to do with him."

"Don't lie to me," Shannon said with a wicked grin. "I saw the way you looked back."

Good thing Shannon hadn't been there when Nick had been carrying on a conversation in Greek with Minister Ramos. Maggie had most assuredly been drooling. "So he's attractive." She turned a page and shook the newspaper straight. "He's also arrogant, controlling, and so uptight he probably sleeps standing."

Shannon laughed. "He'd keep you on your toes." She set her coffee and roll on a nearby ceramic topped table and fanned herself with a manila folder. "I don't know how you can deal with the heat and humidity in this sunroom!"

"Because it's *usually* peaceful. No people. No phones. No demands." But only one orchid. So far. Someday, after Kate finished with college, she'd have time for tables full of any number of exotic plants. "It's just me and some sunshine," Maggie said. She'd hoped for a quiet start to the day, given that her first meeting would be with Nick and Craig to sign an employment agreement. So much for that.

"Exactly," Shannon said, nodding. "You've been so focused on taking care of me and Kate, it's time for you to do something for yourself for a change."

"So I should have an affair?"

"You're always complaining about how every guy you date gets too serious too quickly. That man is exactly what you need," Shannon said, "He won't be whining if you have work to do. He's already got a life."

"That's an excuse for pretending his wife doesn't exist?"

"Maybe she doesn't." Shannon tapped her chin and frowned in concentration. "The talent scout said he was married, but never saw the wife and kids. Maybe it's a front to keep gold diggers off his back. Or maybe his wife was in a terrible, disfiguring accident?"

"Let it go, Shannon. He's not my type."

"Maybe she's a real drag to live with and they're actually separated. Yeah, you don't have to feel guilty about having the affair, Mags." Shannon's eyes brightened. "She's a bitch."

"Where did I go wrong?" Maggie let the newspaper fall onto her lap as she glanced around the solarium, empty except for their chairs and several tables awaiting plants.

"You're no angel." Shannon went on the defensive. "Don't pretend to be one."

Maggie threw the newspaper at her sister. "That's a low blow." True, Maggie had hacked into a bank's checking account system and played with a few balances, namely her own, but that was more than ten years ago. Someone had to pay for her mom's chemo, not to mention Shannon and Kate's clothes and food and the roof over their heads.

Still, the look on their mother's face when Maggie had told her she was going into a juvenile detention center came back in high resolution. "It's jail," her mother had said. "No matter how you look at it."

So what if she'd gotten a suspended sentence by agreeing to help the FBI nail other hackers? The damage had already been done. Maggie had been forced to drop out of high school, her mother's worst nightmare, to work for the Feds and take care of Shannon and Kate. By the time she'd made the best out of a bad situation by starting a security software business, the cancer had won. Her mother was already dead.

Hoping to purge the memories, Maggie padded across the warm flagstone floor and opened the door to the rooftop. She grabbed the bucket she kept outside to accumulate rainwater, poured some into a watering can and proceeded to drench her precious Vanda orchid with its lone fragrant flower.

"Think about it, Mags." Shannon made a project of folding the paper. "No strings. Nick Ballos is *safe*. You know what they say…sweet the sin."

Enough already. "Have you forgotten what it felt like when Craig went out on you?"

"He has nothing to do with this."

Ha! She'd gotten her with that one. "One day you suggested slowing things down with him and seeing other people, and the next day he had a date with another woman."

Shannon's mouth turned down. "He had every right to date someone else. I'd as good as broken it off with him."

"It proved you were right."

"Me? *You* were the one who suggested we were moving too fast."

"You'd just graduated from Georgetown." Maggie shrugged. She set down the container and then sprayed the plant with a heavy mist. "Every woman should spend a few years out of college spreading her wings before settling down. You weren't even engaged yet and his mother was already making wedding plans."

Shannon turned pensive, and, for a split second, it looked as if she might tear up. "I suppose you had a point."

"Am I right, or am I right!" That was Kate's voice. Maggie turned to find her youngest sister standing in the doorway.

Shannon laughed then, a rich, gleeful sound. "You have to admit, Maggie, you say that all the time."

"What is this, rag on Maggie Monday?" Too used to them, she purposefully ignored their jabs. "Kate, what are you doing awake so early?"

Kate stretched, and her black beater inched above her bright green belly button ring. "I'm helping Rufus load the kiln this morning." She brushed a couple chunks of dried clay off her jeans. "He's getting ready for an exhibit next month."

Not for the first time, Maggie worried about Kate's job at the studio. Kate had taken a pottery class the first semester of her senior year in high school and had immediately fallen in love with everything clay. She'd been helping Rufus out ever since, but Maggie wasn't convinced the older man was a good influence.

Kate pulled her hair into a messy ponytail. "Oh, and guess what? He asked me to do some pieces. I get to keep forty percent of my sales. Can you believe it?"

"I thought we agreed you were going to work full-time with Shannon in the office for the summer."

Kate's face fell. "No, Maggie, you agreed. I wanted more hours at the studio."

Shannon shrugged. "I've only got enough work to keep her busy fifteen hours a week. As long as everything gets done, I don't care."

"Fine," Maggie conceded. "Make sure you don't miss orientation later this week." They'd spent years planning this, months touring schools. Their mother would've been so proud of Shannon and Kate, the first women in the family to attend university. And not just any university, either; Kate had been accepted at Georgetown, like Shannon.

"Yeah, sure." Kate turned, and there was something suspect in the way she'd shrugged her shoulders.

"Wait a minute," Maggie said. "Kate, what's going on?" She stopped.

"Kate—"

"I don't think I'm going to orientation." She turned around and crossed her arms.

"Why not?"

"I've talked to people who went and they say it's stupid."

"It's a big day. You need to be there."

"I don't want to go."

"Hey!"

"I'm almost eighteen. I can do whatever I want." On her way out of the greenhouse, Kate slammed the door.

Maggie turned to Shannon. "What was that all about?"

"Have you been listening to her for the last several months?"

"She's always wanted to go to Georgetown."

"That's what you've wanted, Maggie. She's not sure if she wants to go to college anymore."

Their mother had expected Maggie to take care of Shannon and Kate, to keep the sisters together and make sure, first and foremost that they got an education. Maggie had sacrificed way too much only to let her mother's hopes and dreams die this close to the finish line.

"Oh, she's going to college, all right," Maggie said. "I'm not going to let her throw her life away making clay pots."

"It's not your life."

"You know what?" Maggie glared at Shannon. "When you're ready to be mom, dad and bill payer, you can make the decisions around here."

"You know what?" Shannon stood. "Maybe getting

my own apartment wasn't enough. Maybe I should be looking for another job."

"What?" Maggie blinked.

"I need a change. More independence. We better start looking for someone to replace me."

This couldn't be happening. Maggie'd barely gotten used to Shannon getting her own apartment a few months ago. Now this.

"I love you, Maggie, but you and I need some space."

Maggie watched Shannon walk out of the greenhouse, a surreal sense of her world swimming around her. This could not be happening. She was losing them both.

"OKAY, LET'S GET THIS OVER WITH." Nick strode into Maggie's office, coffee cup in hand, and dropped into a chair.

"Good morning to you, too." Maggie stood and rounded her desk.

He gave her a once-over and, to his credit, took in her jean shorts and T-shirt with quiet acceptance. No disdain today, but then, why should she care?

"Morning." He grabbed a pen. "Where do I sign?"

"Hold on," Craig said, following Nick into her office. He stalled uncertainly on seeing Shannon and then continued to the conference table. "There are a few things I need to go through with you two about this employment contract."

Shannon stalked across the room. "Need me for anything, Mags?"

The threats about her sister looking for another job still weighed heavy on Maggie's mind. "Why don't you take a break?"

"Don't need one. I'll be in my office."

Craig watched Shannon leave, and Maggie suddenly felt terrible for having played any part in their split. She'd only been doing what she'd thought was best for Shannon. Maybe she'd been wrong. *You're all they've got now.* How many times in the last ten years had their mother's dying words replayed in Maggie's head?

"Maggie." Nick's voice jolted her back. "You ready?"

"Yep." She turned and caught Craig's gaze. "Thanks for doing this. I appreciate it."

"I'm not the best person for this job," he said, "given I've had prior business dealings with both of you, but this is fairly standard stuff. Let's get this done."

Maggie walked by Nick, caught the scent of fresh air still clinging to his black dress pants and white cotton shirt, and sat down across from the two men. He was still too cocky for her tastes, but at least Mr. Right had left his tie and jacket at home. Where they belonged.

Craig extracted a stack of documents from his briefcase, set several in front of each of them, and set out explaining the terms. He finished with, "All we need is signatures, and you two can have at it."

Without hesitation, Nick flipped to the last page of his copy and signed it. He did the same to the other documents and slid them all over to Maggie. "Is it always this hot in here?" He undid two more buttons at the neck of his shirt and rolled his sleeves.

"The building's central air is out," she said absently, transfixed by the black chest hair and tan skin contrasting with the pure white of Nick's shirt.

"Remind me to bring a fan tomorrow," he said.

A fan? Probably wasn't going to do her any good.

Shaking her head, Maggie turned to the signature page and studied the impatient, yet fluid lines of Nick's handwriting. Putting her own signature next to his seemed too intimate a possibility. A drop of moisture slid down her back. Suddenly, she was sweating like crazy. She held the pen poised, motionless for an instant above the white paper, and sensed Nick's gaze intent on, not her hand, but her face. She glanced up. There was no smile, no give in his expression. They were setting out to work together, but they could have been outright adversaries for all the coolness Maggie felt passing between them.

"Cold feet, Maggie?" Nick's voice was deep and rich. "What are you worried about?"

She couldn't lie to herself and pretend she wasn't attracted to him. Saturday night out on General Walker's verandah, if he'd made a move to touch her, to kiss her, she wasn't sure what she'd have done about it. And now? Right now? She was wondering how his neck would feel on her lips.

Damn him. Did she really need this man?

Unfortunately, yes. Two minutes with the Greek Minister and he'd accomplished what she'd failed to do in four months. Wounded pride or not, she had to sign the contract. For Kate. Even if her kid sister was driving Maggie nuts. Without allowing herself another moment's hesitation, she signed the agreement.

There. Done.

"Well, this is where I cut out, guys."

"We may need you later this week to put together a contract with the Greeks," Nick said.

"I'll fit you in." Craig scooped up the documents. "Happy sailing."

Fully intent on Nick, Maggie was only minimally aware of Craig leaving the room.

"That's that," Nick said, unflinchingly holding Maggie's steady gaze. "Where do we start?"

"First, read through this proposal." She passed it over to him. "We need to get it off to Minister Ramos as soon as possible today."

"Okay."

She picked up one stack of old contracts, trade materials, and other documents she'd been amassing over the weekend for Nick to review and carried them to the coffee table. "Then read all of this." She took over another stack. "And this." She tossed down a thick yellow-and-black manual.

"Whoa. *Hacking for Dummies*," he said, reading the title and then glancing at her. "Is this really necessary?"

"You wanted in on the entire process, right?"

"Right."

"And you have no systems experience, right?"

"Okay. I get it. Where's my office?"

"You're in it. As a matter of fact, you're sitting at your desk." She plugged in an extra phone and set down a cup holder with a handful of pens and pencils. "We have only two offices here. Mine and Shannon's."

"Where's your programming staff?"

"They work offsite and only come in for occasional meetings."

"So be it." Grabbing a pen, he set the proposal in front of him. "I can deal with this for a week."

"I've got news for you, it's going to take a lot longer than that to get you up to speed."

"I'm flying to Athens this weekend."

"You already booked a flight?" This guy was driving her crazy.

He nodded. "Knowing Giannis, he'll look at your proposal today or tomorrow, depending on how soon we get it to him, he'll arrange a meeting for later this week, and he'll want us on-site next Monday."

"Impossible." She'd been planning on this project not getting hot and heavy until *after* Kate started college in about a month.

"Do you want the contract or not?"

"What makes you so sure he'll go with us?"

"I did some digging and got the names of the other companies putting in bids. Giannis doesn't have any ties to any of them. He'll go with a known. Me."

She couldn't imagine spending such a concentrated amount of time in Nick's presence. "You won't be ready."

"Why not, Maggie?" The subtle note of challenge in his voice was, at once, maddening and electrifying. "You have a whole week."

"*I* won't be ready."

"You don't have to go. I'll do it alone."

"Oh, no, you don't." She glared back at him. She didn't know how she was going to manage it with Kate starting school, but Maggie had put too much into this project to back down now. "This is my company, my contract. No matter what, I'm going with you to Greece."

CHAPTER FOUR

"HAVE YOU FOUND ANYTHING?" Nick whispered after placing a call on his cell phone. Although Maggie had left for something to eat, he wasn't sure whether or not Shannon was still at her desk, and these office walls were paper-thin. Sound had a way of carrying louder than the seagulls on Corfu.

"So far, not much," Angelo Bebel said. A friend of Nick's family's with connections he wasn't afraid to use, Angelo had been digging into things back in Greece as a favor to Nick.

"I can't stand this waiting." Nick sat at the couch, tapping his fingertips on the coffee table.

"Relax," Angelo said. "You will break the bow if you keep it always bent."

As a child, Nick had loved listening to Angelo's sayings. Today, he wasn't in the mood. "I'd say waiting five years makes me patient enough."

"Maybe this will make you happy. One of my men managed a picture," he said. "Have you seen my e-mail?"

"No."

"Take a look."

Nick booted up his laptop, opened the e-mail from Angelo, and a grainy photo popped in pieces across his screen. "It's not very clear."

"The best we could get from the distance we were forced to keep. They say few have ever seen this man and lived. Is that him?"

Nick studied the profile, the dramatic lines of the receding hairline, the way the man held his shoulders, his body, and anger, the magnitude of which Nick had only felt once before, flooded through him. "That's him. Dimitri Gavras." The man who'd killed Yanni.

"You sure?"

"Positive."

"His name's not Gavras."

"No surprise there." Nick closed the file. He was getting agitated looking at the man's face, and now wasn't the time.

"It's Berk Tarik."

"What is he, Turkish?"

"Yes. His last known address was in Syria. Damascus."

"Is he a terrorist? Associated with a group?" Nick whispered.

"It appears he plays at it. From all accounts he's only out for the money."

"A mercenary?"

"Too kind a description. From what I can gather, he seems no more than a paid assassin."

"You're sure?"

"Positive."

That meant someone else was ultimately behind Yanni's death. Who and why? Stephano? No. Nick might abhor the man for the way he'd wielded his family's power over Kyrena and the children, but they'd been friends once. Close. He couldn't believe that Stephano would kill his own brother. "Can you find out who hired Tarik?"

"We're working on it, but I'm not sure we can get into their systems. They've got the records wrapped up tighter than a ripe olive in a stone press."

"I can get in. At least I'll try."

"When will you be here?" Angelo asked.

"Next week, if all goes as planned."

The sound of footsteps pounding down a flight of stairs echoed through the thin wall of Maggie's office, and Nick glanced up from his screen. "I have to go. Let me know if you find out anything more."

"That, I will do."

"Maggie? Shannon?" A lanky teenager, dressed in a thin-strapped tank top and cutoff jeans even shorter than Maggie's, came through a side door to the left of Maggie's desk. On seeing him sitting on the sofa, she froze in place. "Who are you?"

He clicked off his cell phone and walked across the room, stretching the stiffness from his limbs. The first thing Nick had done that morning was study Maggie's contract proposal for the Greeks. After he'd suggested a few relatively minor changes in wording and added an addendum relating to the timetable, Maggie had couriered the paperwork to Giannis's embassy office.

Then Nick had spent the rest of the day making his way through the reading material Maggie had accumulated for him. For a body used to much more activity, being forced to sit still at that damned, definitely not ergonomically designed couch all day had been murder.

"Nick Ballos." He extended his hand toward the young woman, hoping to set her at ease. "I'm doing some work for Maggie. May I help you?"

"Yeah, right," the woman said, sarcastically.

"And you are?"

"Sorry." She shook his hand. "Kate. Maggie's sister. Like, where is she, anyway?"

It was hard imagining Maggie with such a young sister, but this teenager somehow fit the bill, and there was no denying the similarities in their features. They both had the same squared-off jawline softened by a delicate chin, the same tentative bow on their upper lip, and the same full cut to the lower one. The only striking difference was the color of their hair. Kate's was dark brown with only flashes of Maggie's rich auburn color.

"Maggie went out for some dinner," he said, realizing she was still waiting for a response. "She should be back fairly soon."

"Shannon?"

"I think I heard her say she was going home for the day." It suddenly occurred to him that other than becoming acutely aware of Maggie's physical features he didn't know much about the woman. Not that he cared, he told himself, but being informed was being armed. "You live upstairs? With your parents?"

"Mom died when I was eight." She went behind Maggie's desk and opened one of the top drawers. "I never knew my father."

That was interesting. "So it's you, Shannon and Maggie?"

"Shannon moved out a few months ago."

"No brothers?"

"Nope." She pushed aside the pencils and pens and Maggie's mess of small wooden puzzles before pulling out a pack of gum and popping a stick in her mouth. "Want some?" She held the pack toward him.

"No, thank you. Who raised you?"

"What is this, twenty questions?" She crushed the gum wrapper and tossed it in the garbage. "Maggie. Duh."

He knew he was pushing it. "How old was she when your mom died?"

Kate's eyes rolled to the ceiling as she did some mental calculations. "Sixteen."

Very interesting. Mother dies at sixteen and you're suddenly caring for two younger sisters. That'd mess with a person's life. Unless their mother had left a big insurance policy, which Nick doubted had been the case, Maggie would've had to get a job, pay bills, take care of things. The information suddenly shed a softer light on Maggie. His initial assessment of her as the tough-as-nails, irresponsible hacker was getting decidedly hacked up.

Then again, they seemed to have made out all right. One comment from Kate didn't necessarily mean he'd been wrong about Maggie. In fact, Nick was rather fond of his perceptions of Maggie the way they were.

The main office door opened and Maggie strode into the room holding a white carryout bag. "Hey, Kate. Looks like you've met Nick."

"Yep." Kate moved out from behind the desk.

"What are you doing tonight?" She set the bag on her desk.

Nick turned away, his head down, and went back to the couch, trying to ignore their conversation.

"I need to unload the kiln," Kate said.

"Rufus's studio again?"

Nick focused on a trade journal article, but their conversation kept distracting him.

"Don't wait up for me." Kate headed for the door. "I'll be home late. Might sleep at the studio, if it gets late."

"Curfew's one," Maggie said in a don't-mess-with-me tone.

"Whatever."

"No, not whatever. One."

The door slammed behind Kate.

Teenagers. Good thing Nick would never have to worry about raising one. He felt Maggie's eyes on him.

"I suppose you'd have handled that differently," she said.

From what he could tell, which wasn't a whole hell of a lot, she appeared to be fighting a losing battle. "I'm no expert, but you gotta let go sometime. Eighteen seems a bit old for orders."

"She's not eighteen. Yet."

"You got me there."

She tossed a white container onto the coffee table. "Figured you'd be hungry."

That surprised him. "Thank you." He flipped open the box to find a roast beef and provolone sandwich, some chips and an apple.

"I had no clue what you'd prefer, so I…"

"Went for boring." He chuckled. She was right. At the moment, as long as the food filled his stomach he didn't care. "It's fine. I appreciate it."

For a moment she looked as if she might carry on a conversation with him, and then, thinking better of it, pulled her own sandwich—loaded with hot peppers, veggies and some green sauce—from the box and ate while checking messages.

He went back to reading. After a short while, the words blurred in front of him, swimming around like the fish he'd seen in the reefs off any number of Greek islands when he was a kid. For years, he hadn't let himself think of Greece, and now he couldn't get the country out of his mind.

He reached for his laptop, clicked on the photo attachment Angelo had sent, and the picture of Dimitri Gavras, Berk Tarik, or whoever the hell he was, filled the screen. He stared at it for several moments, unable to keep himself from reliving the horror of that day five years ago, the day this man had walked into his life and changed everything.

"Nick!" Maggie called out.

Feeling dazed, he glanced over at her.

"I said your name three times," she said. "You okay?"

He nodded.

"How are you doing on all that reading material?"

He assessed the stack. "About halfway through it." That was it. He was shot. He flipped his laptop closed and pushed it aside, wishing he could forget that face. "I gotta get out of here. See you in the morning."

"Night," she said.

He felt her gaze following him as he left the office. Eventually, he'd have to tell her the truth. For now, she didn't need to know anything more than that her job was getting done.

Maggie drove Kate in-fricking-sane. It was all she could do not to scream.

Kate rounded out a big lump of clay and threw it onto the metal plate. Giving the wheel a good couple of kicks, she braced her elbows and centered the mound. Round and round, the wet lump spun until it was smooth and sitting in the exact middle of the potter's wheel.

Kicking again, she formed a dent in the clay and did her best to focus. It'd be a miracle if Kate managed to make anything that looked remotely decent. She should have asked Maggie and gotten it over with.

Pulling the sides of the clay upward, she formed a perfect cylinder. No, she should have *told* Maggie. There was no point in having a discussion with her sister. She never listened, anyway, never left any option for alternative points of view. Maggie didn't ask, she dictated.

"Hey, Kate." Rufus Sherman, master potter and owner of the studio, came into the workshop through the door leading to his apartment. "How you doing today?"

"Fine." Carefully, she put pressure on the top of the cylinder, creating a narrow neck.

"Did you talk to Maggie?"

Bang. The clay collapsed.

"Sorry," Rufus said.

"It's okay." Kate stopped the wheel and straightened. "It was destined to look like shit, anyway."

"You didn't talk to her, did you?"

She shook her head. "Maggie's been really busy with work."

"She's always busy," Rufus said. "I need an answer, Kate."

"I know."

"You want me to talk to her—?"

"No!"

Rufus smiled, understanding flowing from him like a gentle stream. "Takumi can only work through the exhibit, and then he's going back to Japan. That doesn't give me a lot of time to find someone else."

"I'll talk to her this weekend, okay?"

"That works." He headed toward the door. "I'll be back later."

One of the bright fluorescent bulbs overhead buzzed

as Kate stared at the lump of misshapen clay. Did she have anything in her this morning? No way. She cleaned off the wheel. It wasn't every week a girl got to shatter her big sister's dreams.

IT HAD TO BE the nosy-as-all-get-out hacker in her, but Maggie couldn't help herself. The moment Nick left the office, she went to his laptop and booted up the last files he'd been working on, hoping to find out what had turned his mood so suddenly. She couldn't believe he'd left his computer here, but that only showed how distracted he'd become.

Focusing on a cryptic e-mail from someone named Angelo, she opened the related attachment. The photo of a man. He was handsome, but a receding hairline made him look older than he probably was. The picture was grainy, as if taken from a long distance, like surveillance.

What the hell was Nick up to? She had the feeling he was using her and her company for something, but what?

Maggie forwarded a copy of the file to her own system, then covered her tracks and closed down his laptop. She stood and looked for Nick out her window. As the sun set, casting an orangey glow on the outside world, he crossed the street, his strides long and determined. When he reached the parking lot, a black limousine pulled in behind him, almost as if it'd been waiting for him. Two men, hulks, rather, hopped out and glanced around the area. Bodyguards.

A young girl, maybe five years old at most, scooted from the back of the limo and ran, full bore, toward Nick. His posture immediately softened. He scooped her up and leaned his forehead into hers. His daughter. She had to be.

Maggie's gut clenched. His was a young family with so many years ahead of them to spend together. Hers was leaving. Shannon was all but gone and Kate was clawing and scratching her way out the door.

When a woman climbed out of the limo, Maggie barely noticed the young boy with her, most likely their son. The woman was tall, poised, and dressed in a sleeveless white pantsuit. His wife. With long, wavy black hair, she was gorgeous, an ethereal beauty as different from Maggie as night from day.

His daughter still in his arms, Nick leaned over and kissed each of his wife's cheeks. She, in turn, put her hands on either side of his face and caressed his skin in one of the most tender exhibitions of emotions Maggie had ever seen. Mrs. Ballos clearly adored her husband.

Oh, God. Maggie couldn't watch anymore. Quickly, she turned away as an ache of emptiness cinched her chest. Why couldn't she have that, give it? Love, tenderness, devotion. Nick probably had no clue how lucky he was.

"YOU WERE SUPPOSED TO LEAVE this morning," Nick said to Kyrena, smiling despite himself. He'd waited to sign the divorce papers until several months after she and the children had obtained their U.S. citizenship. As of last week, she was free to go and do as she pleased. As was Nick. Finally. Still, he'd been planning on her being gone by now.

He glanced at Carlos. "You shouldn't have come here."

"Don't need to tell me that." Carlos shook his head. "We were heading to the airport, and she refused to leave without saying goodbye."

"The movers were running late, so we had to re-schedule our flight," Kyrena explained, her hands still cradling his face. "I'm glad you told Carlos where you'd be. It's good I can see you one last time. To thank you. For all you've done. *Efkhareesto, polee, ya tee voee-theea sas.*"

"It's nothing Yanni wouldn't have done had I a wife and children who needed help."

Kyrena dropped her hands to her side, looking away to keep from tearing up in front of the children. Christine's arms wrapped around his neck, nearly strangling him. "I don't want to go, Uncle Nick."

"Chrissy, *meekros tarta,* you'll love California. Sunshine. Ocean. Warm all the time. And your mom said you can finally get a puppy."

"I don't care about a dog." Her brow furrowed and her eyes misted with tears. "I'm going to miss you."

"You'll be busy making new friends. You won't have time to miss me."

"Will you come and see us? Promise?"

He hesitated. How could he make promises with a future as uncertain as his? How could he let her down? "I promise."

Nestor stood next to his mother, staring at the ground. Nick set Chrissy down and knelt by Nestor as a tear trailed down the boy's cheek. Nestor had taken the death of his father harder in some ways than Kyrena. He wouldn't get into a car for months afterward and woke with nightmares about explosions for years. Unfortunately, Nick could identify. It wasn't until Kyrena had come to Baltimore with the children, that Nestor had slowly, surely learned to laugh again.

He pulled Nestor into his arms, felt the boy's grip tighten. "It's going to be okay, Nestor."

"I know." He pulled back, clearly trying to be strong.

"You'll be near my parents." With Kyrena's mother dying long before they'd left Greece, Nick's mom and dad had been the closest thing to grandparents the children had ever had.

"That'll be good," Nestor said. "But I'm worried I might never see you again."

Nestor and Chrissy were the only connections making Nick think twice about going to Greece, but Carlos would be with them. The man was, for all intents and purposes, their father, and would soon be in reality.

"I'll call," Nick said. "We'll talk."

"Promise?"

"Promise."

"Bye, Nick." Nestor hugged him one last time. And Nick felt Carlos rub the boy's head.

After another hug for Chrissy, Kyrena ushered the children back into the limo. "I'll be right back," she told them before closing the door and turning to Nick. She frowned and poked him in the chest. "Don't do anything stupid now, okay?" This was about as angry as Kyrena managed. "Promise me, you'll get on with your life. Please."

More promises. Good thing this one he could keep. Getting on with his life meant going back to Greece. "I promise."

"Find a woman, Nick. Have children. Make a life with her. There is someone out there for you." She paused, took a necklace from under her blouse and drew the long chain over her head. "And when you find her give this to her." She put the Heart of Artemis in his hand.

"I can't take this."

"And I can't keep it." She glanced at Carlos and

smiled. "Did you know that Yanni's mother gave the exact pendant to both Yanni and Stephano?"

"No. I didn't."

"She told them that it holds the key to life and they would know what to do with it." She closed Nick's fingers around the heavy gold chain. "I think Yanni would want you to have it."

He glanced at the necklace before stuffing it in his pocket.

"Come and visit as soon as we're settled. Okay?"

He nodded.

She squeezed his arm, climbed back into the limo, and Nick shut the door so he could talk to Carlos.

"See ya, Nick," Carlos said, reaching for the front door.

Nick stopped him. "I know you've done everything in your power to make sure this move isn't traceable, but I need to warn you." He drew Carlos away from the limo. "There may be renewed interest in Kyrena and the children's whereabouts."

"We haven't noticed any tails for years." Carlos straightened. "What's up all of a sudden?"

Nick looked away.

"Dammit, Nick—"

"Lower your voice. I don't want Kyrena to hear."

"You're going to Greece." Carlos shook his head. "That's going to stir the pot again. I can't believe it. When?"

"Next week."

"You couldn't wait a month or two?"

"You were supposed to be gone by now."

Carlos glared at him.

"I've already waited five years for this." Nick glared back. "With the sale of the company, I've taken care of

Kyrena and the kids' financial worries. And now that they're American citizens, they don't need me anymore. From here on out, it's your responsibility, Carlos, to keep them safe."

"If she finds out I knew you were going to Greece, she'll kill me."

"And if you tell her she won't leave." Nick stepped back. "Do you want to marry her or not?"

Shaking his head, Carlos climbed back into the car. Nick stood there until the limo, with the kids' hands waving out the windows, disappeared from sight. An hour or so later, he pulled onto his gated drive, past the main house waiting to be sold, its interior dark and still, and parked at the carriage house hidden in the woods.

Normally, Chrissy and Nestor would run out to meet him, or already be hanging out at his place, watching TV. Not tonight. His small, normally bustling house was silent. He flicked on a few lights, the TV, but it soon became evident that no amount of ambient noise was going to crowd out the growing emptiness inside him.

Nick threw his keys on the granite counter, along with the Heart of Artemis pendant and chain, heard the hollow sound echo through the house, and that's when it hit him. He'd been so focused on keeping them safe, on helping them start their new lives, and on him going back to Greece, he hadn't realized how much he was going to miss Nestor and Chrissy.

CHAPTER FIVE

"I THINK WE NEED another programmer." Braiding a chunk of hair from the top of her head, Maggie sat at her desk talking on the phone with one of her developers about the contract with Greece. No matter how she tried occupying her mind, she kept coming back to the gorgeous hunk of conceited, uptight, out-of-reach man directly in her line of vision.

For two long days, she'd been stuck watching Nick, right there, smack dab in front of her, and she had his habits down, knew his every quirk with absolute precision. If he was working on his laptop, he'd lean forward, his back ramrod straight, rest his elbows on his knees and tap his right index finger on the indent above his upper lip. One, two, three times. Stop. Then again. And he was still wearing dress pants and collared shirts to the office, despite the one-hundred-plus temperatures outside.

The most relaxed he ever got was when he was reading. He'd sit back on the couch or chair and prop his long, muscular legs onto the coffee table, occasionally shifting his weight from side to side with deep, quiet sighs. Almost every hour, on the hour, he'd stand and stretch his back and neck out, first leaning left, then right, then forward and backward, forward and backward. Always breathing slowly. So slowly. Controlled.

Calm. As if he had all the time in the world. As if nothing ever troubled him. While she was treated to the full length of his gorgeous profile.

Married, she'd reminded herself, over and over. And *safe* as Shannon had so adroitly pointed out.

Maggie supposed that was why she'd allowed herself to fantasize about him, imagining kissing him, having sex with him. She envisioned walking over to him, right now, throwing his paperwork aside, pushing him back down on the couch, climbing on top of him, and proving to him just how messy life could get. Life with her anyway.

The worst of it all? He acted as if she didn't exist. Which was, she supposed, a good thing. As if she didn't have enough to worry about planning for the second biggest contract in her company's history. She should've made him share Shannon's office.

Maggie spun around in her chair and made herself look out the window. "If we get the contract," she continued, "they're going to want it done yesterday."

Usually, work was a breeze when compared to her personal life, but she wasn't prepared for this project to move as fast as Nick expected, not with Kate's orientation this week. If Nick was right, they did get the contract and Maggie found herself in Greece next week, how was she going to get Kate ready to head off to college?

"Do I get to manage this one?" Alex, her lead developer, asked.

That would solve her whole problem, but Alex wasn't quite ready. "Not the whole project, but maybe parts of it," she said, hedging. She'd get the A-Team settled in Athens. Once she got them going, she might be able to alternate her time between home and Greece until Kate started school. It'd mean a lot of traveling, but Shannon could stay with Kate while Maggie was out of town. "I'll be flying back and forth between here and Athens, so I'll need you to hold down the fort from time to time."

"Well, if you're going to make me hang in Greece for a month, we gotta have Allen."

"That's still not enough manpower. I won't be doing much detailed programming on this one, Alex."

"I'm telling ya, the A-Team's all over this one, Maggie. No sweat."

Behind her, Nick's chair creaked. He must be stretching. And, no, she was not going to look. Lodging the phone between her shoulder and ear, she grasped her watering can and walked around her desk to dampen the African violet pot. "What about Stephen? He's good." She snipped off a few dead leaves with her fingernails.

"He hooked up with the lead singer in some heavy metal chick band. No way is Stephen going to leave the country for a month."

"I already talked to him. He's onboard."

"Not cool, Maggie." Alex sounded so depressed. "We won't be the A-Team anymore."

She tried her best not to laugh. "Did you know Stephen's last name is Asher. Alex, Allen, and Asher. You're all set, dude."

"Tight. Stephen rocks, but I'm not sharing a bedroom with him. He snores like a manic disk drive."

"I'll make sure there's an extra room. You're prepared to leave this weekend, if we have to?"

"All set."

"The new A-Team it is."

"Let me know as soon as you get the word," Alex said. Maggie hung up the phone.

"I'm starving," Nick said, standing. And, of course,

stretching that tall, lean body of his. "Think I'll head out for something to eat. You hungry?"

She refused to watch him walk away. "Sure, grab me a sandwich."

"Anything in particular?"

"I'm easy."

"Sure you are." He stopped, looked down at the carpet, and sighed. "I'm sorry. I shouldn't have said that."

Huh? Her guard flew up, not to mention her head.

"We're going to be working together for a while, and I'd appreciate doing it without the snipping back and forth." He glanced back at her, as genuine as she'd ever seen a man. "Can we call a truce?"

Honestly, she didn't know what to say.

"I can be mature, if you can."

Put that way, she felt petty for hesitating. "Sure. Why not?"

"Good. That's good." Nodding, he took off for the elevators and food, leaving her to contemplate the situation.

Why? She sat back. What was he after? A truce sounded professional enough, like the right thing to do, harmless, tame even. All the same, somehow, some way, Maggie had a hunch she'd end up with the short end of the stick.

"NOT BAD FOR A BEGINNER," Maggie said, reading the code Nick had typed on his screen. With evening fast approaching, she was sitting on the couch next to him, guiding him through some hands-on programming, and, Nick could tell, carefully guarding her words.

Good thing, too. She was, oddly enough, too damned sexy when she snipped at him, and that inane truce he'd suggested earlier this afternoon had been the only thing he could think of to save what was left of his sanity. His head felt as if it might explode.

Since Monday morning, he'd spent almost thirty hours buried in reading material and working through programming tutorials. He'd learned an entire foreign language in three very long days. Filtering, monitoring, tracing, blocking. Firewalls, back doors, router encryption. The list went on and on.

Sitting in the same office with Maggie the entire time hadn't helped matters. He'd get distracted by her talking on the phone. She had the habit of leaning back in her chair and fussing with her hair, first twisting it, then braiding sections, then bunching it together and piling it on top of her head. The motions offset her beautifully shaped arms and the multicolored butterfly tattooed on the inside of her wrist.

The only thing worse was when she left her desk and walked from one potted plant to the next, leaning over in her jean shorts and tight-fitting T-shirts while she watered her plants, fussed with their stems or leaves, or loosened the soil. She was a bit of a pixie, but had the most perfectly proportioned legs he'd ever seen on a woman.

As if having to endure the sensual sights wasn't bad enough, he was constantly buffeted with the sound of her voice either on the phone or talking with Shannon or Kate, first soft and calculating, then sarcastic and strong. Her business tactics were as different from his as light from dark. Where he might've approached a problem from a quiet analytical standpoint with solutions and timetables, she charged like a bull, first joking and coaxing, then expecting and insisting. From the looks of her financials, whatever she was doing was working.

"Try taking that code and revising it to allow remote access," she suggested.

He inserted a string he thought might work. "How's that?"

"Pretty good," Maggie said, "if what you want is to send up a flag to every hacker with a keyboard and a few free megs to give your system a shot."

She was close to Nick. Too close. He could smell her hair, or at least the fruity scent of her shampoo, every time she leaned toward him and pointed at the code streaming across his laptop.

Like now. Right in front of him. Every auburn strand exploded with color. Would it feel as warm and soft as it looked, or was expectation nine-tenths of attraction? What would she do if he took her hair in his hands, pulled it to his face and inhaled?

He had no doubt she was attracted to him. She'd made that apparent by the quickening of her breath whenever he'd been near her the past two days, by the way she pulled away her hand at the barest touch of his skin. Sometimes she would focus on him so intently, he felt as if he might burst into flames. Of course when he'd glance over at her, she'd look away.

Cat and mouse. She had to be waiting for him to do something about it. Unfortunately, now was not the time for a fling.

"Yo, Nick?" She glanced back at him. "You in there somewhere?"

"Sorry." While the truce was helping, this hands-on stuff wasn't working at all. All he wanted his hands on was her. He had to stay focused on Greece. On getting access to those secure files. On finding Berk Tarik and whoever hired him. "Okay," he said. "What'd I do wrong?"

"You copied the code, right?"

"Yeah."

"And that system allows access—"

"So, by default, I'd be allowing it, too."

"Exactly." She grinned and leaned back against the couch. The movement shifted her infinitesimally closer to him. "I hate to feed your ego, but you catch on pretty fast."

Yeah, he was catching on, all right, to how sexy she was. He never would have guessed jeans and a T-shirt could turn him on. The shorts fit her gently curving hips, offsetting her bare legs. And the stre.chy fabric of her T-shirts, despite today's juvenile saying *I fought the lawn and the lawn won* clung to her breasts in the way a primly pressed cotton shirt could only dream about.

"Maggie…" He glanced at her lips, her eyes. Bad idea. "Show me how you hack into a secure system." That would redirect his attention. He needed to be ready for any opportunity that might present itself.

"Why?"

"If I'm to understand system vulnerability, I need to get a feel for possible attacks."

"Okay." She slid his laptop in front of her. "Let's pick something simple. How 'bout a mailing database from…let's say an animal humane society. Probably not too secure a system. We might be able to get in."

She found a Web site from a small town in the Midwest and sent bugged e-mails to several employees with fake requests for information. "Once you get a response, you can get their IP address. Once you have the address, you have what you need to break in. Here we go."

He watched her intently, following most of what she was doing, but didn't want to interrupt to ask questions. That would've pulled her out. Once Maggie began typing, she was a machine, as if she'd entered an alternative world, and her brain sunk into the code. For a while, it was almost as if she didn't breathe. She seemed to forget where she was, forgot he was sitting next to her.

Even he lost track of the time. Minutes turned into an hour. He could see how days might turn into nights, nights into weeks, and hackers could lose hold of their lives. Then, he saw the opening she created on the screen, and it was as if she were taking them through a cyber doorway.

"There," she said. "We're in." A file of names and addresses spilled across his screen.

"Amazing." He wasn't sure he could ever duplicate the results. "How did you learn to do that?"

"I took a Web site design class in junior high. Before I knew it, I was doing sites for teachers, or their spouses with businesses." She shrugged and rubbed the butterfly tattoo on the inside of her wrist. "From there you learn code. Kids pick it up easily. It helped my mom pay the bills. Before you know it, I met a few hackers online. I was curious. One thing led to another."

"Then your mom got sick."

She glanced at him, surprise registering. "Who told you?"

"Kate."

She circled the tattoo over and over again with her thumb.

He reached over and stilled her hand. "Did you get that for your mom?"

Maggie nodded. "She loved butterflies."

A remembrance. He couldn't think of a better reason for getting a tattoo.

"When Shannon and I were young, we'd go to the

park with a butterfly net and bring them home in a big plastic container." Maggie smiled. "She'd admire them for a few minutes, tell us all about them, show us in a book their caterpillar form, and then let them fly away out the apartment window."

She grinned. "I remember finding a Cecropia caterpillar on an apple tree branch. We brought it home, and Mom went crazy. She borrowed a cat carrier from a neighbor and put the branch inside. We all watched it lace itself into a cocoon, and then, since they're overwintering, us kids forgot all about it. Not my mom. She sprayed it with a fine mist every so often all winter long and in the spring set it in the sunlight.

"One day, out of the blue, it cracked out of its cocoon," Maggie continued, her eyes widening, sparkling with a memory. "And it was the most wondrous thing I've ever seen. Their wing spans are five to six inches, their bodies are big and furry, and they're *so* beautiful."

"What did you do with it?"

"Shannon, Kate and I wanted to keep it, but Mom let it go that night." She sat back and sighed. "She was always doing cool stuff."

He stretched his arms out along the back of the couch and relaxed, ready to listen with no ulterior motives other than simply wanting to know. Maybe they could take this truce one step further, become friends, and he could stop thinking about her locking lips with him. "Your mom sounds amazing."

"You have no idea." Maggie looked away, was silent for a moment. "She got pregnant with me when she was in high school. Divorced my dad before Kate was born. I haven't seen him since, so Mom was on her own with us kids.

"Right away, she became the manager of the apartment building we lived in and worked as a night janitor at an office complex. An old neighbor lady used to sleep at our apartment while she was gone. She'd come home in the morning, get us off to school, take care of building management issues, and have supper waiting for us when we got home."

Maggie sat back and crossed her legs on the couch. "I swear, she lived on three hours of sleep. She never stopped. Baking cookies, doing laundry, a slave driver when it came to homework. When I look back, life must have been a pretty stark reality for her.

"The only real vacation I ever remember taking was right before she got sick. She splurged and took a whole week off one summer and we rented a cottage near Ocean City. A cute little place with the ocean right out our back door. I remember feeling rich, like royalty. Met a cute boy at the beach, too. He bought me an ice cream cone. That was the summer I found out I'd never be allowed to date."

"Never?"

"Ever. For my entire life." Maggie laughed. "She didn't want to take the chance we'd get pregnant, like her." She sobered. "Ruining her life. She never graduated from high school, didn't have time for her GED.

"Her dream was for all of her girls to go to college. She talked about it all the time, had some savings for each one of us. When we had to use the money to pay her medical expenses, it almost killed her." Maggie paused and looked down at her hands. "If I'm half as good a woman as she was, I'll be doing okay."

"I'd say you're doing a pretty good job."

"Tell that to Kate."

"How did your mom die?"

"Pancreatic cancer. Fast. Deadly. Painful."

"I'm sorry."

"I've had a lot of time to get over it."

"When you lose someone you love, time doesn't matter. I don't care what anyone says, the loss sticks with you forever."

"Who did you lose?"

"Yanni Kythos. My best friend."

"He's why you haven't been back to Greece, isn't he?"

Nick nodded and looked away. It was all well and good that she'd wanted to share, but that didn't mean he needed to reciprocate. Maybe this whole truce thing hadn't been such a good idea. Before she could dig any deeper, he said, "So, who would you be, what would you be doing, if your mom hadn't died?"

She smiled. "Believe it or not, I'd probably live in the country and have a nursery, raising plants and trees. And orchids. I sure as hell wouldn't be programming."

"You sure?"

"Kate didn't tell you that part, eh?" She laughed. "I hacked into several bank systems and stole money to pay Mom's medical bills. When the FBI caught me, they offered me a deal. Help with programming their security system, or go to jail."

"No kidding?" Maggie was a survivor, so this news didn't surprise him. The fact that she was telling him did.

"I don't kid about the FBI."

"Made you who you are today."

"For better or worse." She put her head down, almost as if she was ashamed.

"Hey. You didn't have a choice. You did what you had to do to take care of your family." He paused. "Sometimes we have to do wrong to make things right."

"Mom didn't look at it that way."

"She would've been worried about you. Not herself."

"Wow." She stared at him. "I never would've guessed you, of all people, would bend those kind of rules."

"When the situation involves someone I love," he said, looking directly into her eyes, "I'll bend…or break…anything."

He would've sworn she moved toward him. Then again, maybe he'd moved toward her. Good thing his cell phone took that moment to ring, breaking the spell. "Nick Ballos," he said, flicking it open.

"This is Minister Ramos's assistant," a pleasant-sounding woman said with a distinctive Greek accent. "He wants to schedule a meeting to discuss contract terms tomorrow. Is there a time that works best for you and your staff?"

"A Thursday meeting with Giannis to discuss terms." He glanced at Maggie, covered the mouthpiece with his hand. "They want to meet in the morning. What time works best?"

She grinned and flashed ten fingers.

"Ten o'clock."

"Very good," Giannis's assistant said. "Until then." Nick disconnected the call.

"Woohoo!" Maggie said. "We're on."

MAGGIE DIALED Kate's cell phone for the gazillionth time that night. Finally, her sister answered. "Yeah, what's up?" Kate said.

"I've got an important appointment in the morning, so I won't be able to go with you to orientation." Normally, Maggie would've automatically rescheduled the orientation at Georgetown without consulting Kate, but Shannon's admonishments had been hanging in the back of her mind. "Shannon said she would go, or I can call and reschedule."

"No sweat. I'll go alone."

"You need an adult ther—"

"No, Maggie, I *don't* need an adult. I'm old enough to do this on my own."

"You should have someone with you."

"It's not a big deal. I've got all the paperwork. I can handle it."

"You should—"

"Maggie. I can handle it. Bye."

Click.

CHAPTER SIX

"Put your jacket back on," Nick said.

"It's hot out." D.C.'s midsummer sun beating down on her head, Maggie walked beside Nick down the Massachusetts Avenue sidewalk on their way to their morning meeting at the Greek embassy. She swung said suit coat over her shoulder with a defiant flick of her wrist.

He stopped and looked down at her. "You have no idea how men see you, do you?"

"As a woman? Wow, there's a news flash." She couldn't help being snotty. The tentative connection they'd made last night in her office—talking about her mom and his friend—had her, for some reason, feeling skittish. The guy might be safe, and a truce was all well and good, but there was no point in getting too close. And she certainly wasn't about to change how she behaved to better fit in with his crowd.

"Truce, remember?" Like a disapproving father figure, he looked down at her. "Do you want this contract or not?"

"There's nothing wrong with what I'm wearing."

"I didn't say there was anything *wrong* with it. It's just that…in that sleeveless thing. With you…your…" He opened his mouth and flung out his hands as if he couldn't find the right wording. "Hair coloring."

Hair coloring?

"Half the men on Giannis's staff won't be able to take their eyes off you."

"Are you serious?"

"Look, when you dress in jean shorts and T-shirts, men can…can…dismiss someone as beautiful as you."

Did he just call her beautiful?

"When you look this sexy, these conservative Greek men will completely lose sight of the fact that you're *supposed* to be a professional."

She glanced down at the stretchy blouse she was wearing. She'd bought it because the green and cream colored print matched her suit. The fact that it went well with her fair skin and red hair, and had a funky twist of fabric gathering slightly below her cleavage were added bonuses.

Maggie bit her tongue and slipped on her suit coat. She might be stubborn, but she wasn't stupid. If presenting a more conservative image was what it would take to get this contract, then conservative she'd be. Why not go one step further? She pulled a clip out of her purse and gathered her hair at the back of her head. "There," she said. "How's that?"

"You're fine," he said without glancing back.

"Look at me." When this was all over, she was going to give Nick Ballos a piece of her mind.

He stopped on the steps, turned and scrutinized her appearance. "You look perfect. For this meeting." The serious expression he'd plastered to his face finally softened. "Personally, I prefer you in jeans and T-shirts." He spun around and continued toward the entrance.

She didn't know how his wife could stand him. "So you can dismiss me?"

He stopped, and without turning said, "Truce or not, I don't think I'll ever be able to dismiss you."

What the hell was that supposed to mean?

Maggie shook her head and followed him into the Greek embassy, blue-and-white striped flags flapping in the breeze above their heads. Cool, stale air hit her in the face the moment they entered the old building. Sound echoed off the walls in the cavernous foyer.

They introduced themselves at the front reception area and were escorted to a waiting area upstairs. Nick sat down in one of several chairs. "Might as well get comfortable. Everyone's always late in Greece."

"We're in America."

"This embassy is considered Greek soil. They'll be late."

Maggie crossed her legs and flipped through a magazine. People filed in sporadically, presumably heading to their offices. At least ten minutes later, Maggie glanced up to find Giannis Ramos stepping off the elevator.

"Nick!" The minister extended his arms.

Nick shook his hand and kissed each of the other man's cheeks.

"Miss Dillon." He nodded at her. "It's a pleasure."

"Good morning, Minister," she said.

"Well, let's get down to business. I have to catch a flight home this afternoon."

Giannis led them to a conference room where several people—none of them women—had already gathered. Introductions were made and, as it turned out, Maggie was glad Nick had recommended she keep on her jacket. The men on Giannis's staff were young and definitely eyeing her. The meeting took several hours. Nick fielded several of the questions quite well, but there was no doubt Maggie's expertise impressed Giannis's team.

As the meeting drew to a close, Nick stood up. "We'll draw up a contract as you've requested and present it this afternoon."

"Very good." Giannis stood and signaled for his staff to leave.

"Can Shannon help with the changes?" Nick quietly asked as the group left the conference room.

"I'll call her," Maggie said. "And Craig."

"No. Absolutely not."

"Shannon, I need you," Maggie whispered, gripping her cell phone tightly in her hand. "Nick was right. They're ready for actual contracts. Craig's on his way to our office to draft them, but he's going to need your help."

She'd known Shannon would resist working so closely with Craig, but she hadn't realized how vehement her sister would be. They'd been arguing ever since Maggie had finished their meeting with Giannis's group. Afterward, Nick and Giannis had left for lunch, leaving her to get the contracts drafted.

Really, she didn't mind. She felt a bit like a third wheel around those two. Now, she was pacing back and forth in the cubicle Giannis had said she could use outside his office, and she and Shannon were back to square one.

"You can relay everything directly to Craig," Shannon said. "You don't need me."

"I don't have time to recreate the wheel here. I need you to pull some old contracts from our files for terms and verbiage. Craig's going to use them as a starting point."

"He's completely capable of figuring it out by himself. That's what you pay him for, isn't it?"

"We don't have the time to volley revisions back and forth. We need this done right the first time." Maggie paused, collecting her patience for one final push. "Craig is doing us a favor by giving us priority. It would take me forever to drive to our office and then back here. You know these contracts inside and out. Burying the hatchet for a few hours isn't going to kill you."

"Easy for you to say."

"Shannon, this is it. We've got to get Minister Ramos a contract this afternoon, so he can get it approved ASAP by his legal department. Please?" Silence hung between them like a teetering tightrope walker. Maggie couldn't stand it. "Shannon, I need you now like I've never needed you before."

"You know this is nothing short of torture for me, right?" Shannon's heavy sigh, music to Maggie's ears, sounded across the line. "This evens the score for all the times you took me to the doctor, teacher conferences, tutoring—"

"I get the idea." Maggie grinned into the receiver. "One more thing?"

"What?" Shannon snapped.

"Can you please, pretty please with hot fudge, pecans, *and* caramel on top, wait to look for another job until this Greek project is finished?"

Shannon hesitated. "I wasn't looking anyway."

"Good. You want the FBI account—"

"Yes!"

"It's yours. Glad to have that settled." And it felt settled, too. Maybe someday Shannon could take over the whole company and Maggie would…would…who knew what she'd do? It didn't matter.

"So…" Shannon's tone changed. "What's it like hanging out with Nick?"

"He's a co-worker, that's all." Maggie wasn't sure who she was trying to convince of that obvious lie, Shannon or herself.

"You are so dead." Shannon laughed. "Well, enjoy the camaraderie while you can. Problems await your return tonight."

"What problems?"

"I shouldn't tell you this."

"Let me guess," Maggie said, already suspicious. "Kate, right?"

"She didn't go to the orientation today. Said she had to work."

"Rufus probably had some crisis only Kate could handle."

"Yup. It's not the end of the world, Maggie."

"I know. I'll call the school and reschedule."

"Have you ever thought that you might be going through some weird kind of empty nesting issue?"

"At twenty-six? Get real. And I'm the sister, not the mom."

"You were taking care of us long before Mom died." Shannon got quiet on the phone. "You've done all you can, Mags. Let her go."

"Yeah, right." Maggie felt more of her control slipping away. *I'm sorry, Mom. I'm doing the best I can.*

"His highness is here," Shannon said, her tone changing yet again. She put Maggie on speaker.

"Hey, Craig," Maggie said. "Thanks for doing this."

"Let's get this done with," Craig said, "so I can get out of here."

Maggie had Shannon pull various old contracts and

explained to Craig the provisions that needed to be added and changed to tailor the agreement for this project. It took the three of them more than an hour to finish. "Can you e-mail me the contracts?"

"Already done," Craig said.

"I owe you," Maggie said, hanging up the phone. She was printing out the paperwork when Nick and Giannis returned from lunch.

"How's it going?" Nick asked, stepping into the cubicle.

"Done."

"Really?"

"Really." She took a deep breath and handed the contract to him. "Will you please review it?"

He sat down and read the contract while referring to his own notes. Maggie leaned back in her chair and closed her eyes. She had no idea how much time had passed when she heard Nick whisper her name. "Maggie." When she opened her eyes, he was watching her. "It looks great."

"Good."

Nick stood and she followed him into Giannis's office. "Here's your contract."

As Nick handed the paperwork to Giannis, Maggie was almost giddy with relief. The day couldn't have gone any better, and Nick had been exactly what she'd needed to make this project happen.

"Very good." Giannis set the contract on his desk and walked them toward the exit. "Your team can start this project next week, correct?"

Maggie nodded.

"Absolutely," Nick said.

"Then we'll let you know our decision by the end of the day tomorrow." Giannis shook their hands. "And with any luck, you'll be coming to the dinner party Marie and I are having this weekend. She'll be so happy to see you after all these years."

"It'll be wonderful to see her again."

"I must warn you now, though." Giannis patted him on the back. "Marie ran into Talia, Stephano's wife, the other day and felt inclined to invite them to the dinner party. I hadn't told her you might be in town."

"And you still wish for me to come?"

"He's bound to find out you're in town. The sooner you break the ice, the better."

They said goodbye to Giannis, left the cold, air-conditioned entrance of the embassy building, and stepped outside into hot and muggy D.C. air.

"Stephano," Maggie said. "That's—"

"The brother of my friend who died."

There was bad blood there, no doubt. The steely edge to his voice made Maggie hope he never got that angry with her. "Is this going to affect my project?"

"Absolutely not. Your job won't be impacted."

"This really might happen." Maggie did everything possible to contain herself. This job would pave the way for projects with other Mediterranean countries and large U.S. corporations. Paying for Kate's college wouldn't be a problem.

"It's going to happen," Nick said. "We're going to be in Greece next week."

If only everything was working out as well with Kate.

"Can I buy you a drink?" Nick asked, out of the blue.

Surprised, Maggie glanced up at him. He looked as if he didn't want to go home, a feeling she understood.

Her apartment had been awfully quiet these days with Shannon living off on her own and Kate half out the door. "What the hell. Sure."

MOMENTS LATER, they walked into the first-floor lounge of a large hotel a few blocks from the Greek embassy building. To his great relief, Maggie passed up the quiet, intimate tables for two set within a dark and intimate alcove for a stool at the bar.

She ordered a *mojito* and he a Chivas on the rocks. They talked about the day's meetings and possible alternatives for travel. Their drinks had no sooner been set in front of them, than she turned fully toward him and said, "So, tell me about him."

He glanced warily over at her. "Who?"

"Yanni Kythos."

Damn. He swallowed a hefty gulp of whiskey.

"It's your turn to spill." Her eyebrow arched, as if to challenge him. "I spilled last night."

It seemed only fair, but then he'd never talked about this with anyone, not even Kyrena. He swirled the ice chunks in his glass. "How does one explain twenty years of friendship and brotherhood?"

"Try."

Nick searched for the words that might explain the essence of what Yanni had meant to him. "I was an only child and...different."

"Different from what?"

"Most other kids," he said as the sound of a live piano mingled softly with the conversations in the bar. "I was extremely quiet. My mother said I didn't speak until I was four, and even then my words were few and far between. My early elementary teachers thought there was something wrong with me, that I should be in some kind of special ed program."

The show of protectiveness on her face made him smile. Maybe she wasn't such a tough cookie, after all. "Don't worry. My mom and dad ignored them. They knew who I was, and they knew when we moved to Greece, it would be hard for me. I was seven. Tall and skinny and awkward as hell, but the ambassador position was my father's dream."

Nick thought of that first day off the plane, remembered it like yesterday. The smells of a hot sun in a big city, food vendors on the corners, taxis honking. "We stayed in Athens, until my parents found a house at the shore. They made sure we'd be near many other children, hoping I'd make lots of friends. I made one, the only one who mattered."

"Yanni?"

He nodded, folding a napkin and wiping off the moisture droplets on his glass. "That first day on the beach, I was building a sand castle when he ran up to me, full of energy, full of questions. What's your name? Where are you from? What're you doing? Can I help with the sand castle? I never answered. I watched and listened. I learned Greek from him in a matter of a few months. I thought he was the most fascinating person I'd ever known. Like a toy top, Yanni never stopped moving, talking, laughing, playing.

"He was a small kid with a personality as big and bright as the sun. Everyone loved Yanni, but I still can't figure out why he chose me as his best friend."

"You complemented each other."

"It was much more than that, hard to put into words. I suppose that even as young boys, we understood the world was full of duplicity. We trusted each other. Knew each of us would die for the other. He and I never fought. Not once. Even his brother, Stephano, eventually turned on Yanni."

"Let me guess." She held out her hand. "A woman."

He laughed. "Isn't there always?"

"Of course." She grinned. "So there were only two boys in his family?"

Nick nodded. "Yanni was the oldest, so his father's expectations were great. The Kythos family was, is still, one of the wealthiest, most powerful families in Greece. Eventually, everyone thought, Yanni would inherit everything.

"Instead, he turned down his family's fortune and struck out on his own. With me. We worked our asses off, built a shipping company from scratch, and were doing very well when he was killed." Nick paused. The whole truth would only bring on more questions. "In a car accident. Not long after his father died and left everything to Stephano." Nick couldn't keep the disgust from his voice.

"You hate his brother."

"Hate's a strong word. I dislike and distrust him."

"Stephano is why you haven't been back?"

"We've had our disagreements over the years. He's made it difficult for me to be there."

"And now?"

"I don't give a rat's ass about the man. Or Greece. But I still feel the ache of losing Yanni. Like I'm missing an essential piece of myself." He finished his drink. "That enough *spilling* for you?"

Maggie looked at him with dawning understanding and set aside her empty glass. "I need to get home."

"Tomorrow's going to be a big day." He followed her outside, into the early evening stillness.

"You sound so sure they're going to approve the contract," she said.

"If I were you, I'd start packing for Greece." He walked her to her car. "By the way, earlier…this morning…I didn't… You looked nice today."

"Are you saying I don't look nice every day?"

"You know what I mean."

"Yeah, I do." She smiled. "Thanks."

Nick turned toward his own car at the other end of the lot. Though he was still not quite ready to go home, there was nowhere else to go, no one else to call. He'd lived in the D.C. Baltimore area for close to ten years and Maggie was the person he felt most comfortable around.

THE SMELL OF BURNING LEATHER got him every time.

Not this dream again. Nick tossed and turned. *Dimitri Gavras. Berk Tarik. Assassin. Murderer. No. Wake up. Wake up!* He rolled over in bed and opened his eyes. Every detail of that day five years ago in Athens came back to him as if it were happening all over again. He'd known the moment he'd met Tarik. He should've never let Yanni get in that car.

Tossing back sheets soaked with sweat, Nick sat up in bed and flicked on the lamp. He steadied his breathing and glanced down at the scars dotting the smooth surface of his upper arm, shoulder and chest. He fingered them lightly, then rubbed harder and harder, hoping to take away the pain. The anger. The guilt. It was his fault. As young boys—blood brothers—he and Yanni had vowed to protect each other against any and all dangers. Only Nick had failed.

The house was quiet. Too quiet. Too still.

I'm sorry, Yanni. I'll make it right.

CHAPTER SEVEN

KATE LAY IN BED, listening to the quiet sounds of Maggie poking around in the kitchen. Already, it was Friday morning. She'd told Rufus she'd give him an answer this weekend, but waiting another day or two wasn't going to change anything.

Do it. Now. Quit being such a girl.

Her heart beating unevenly, Kate swung her feet to the floor, opened her bedroom door and headed toward the kitchen. "Maggie?"

"Hey. You're up early." Already going a mile a minute, Maggie poured herself a cup of coffee, put a piece of bread in the toaster and started unloading the clean dishes from the dishwasher. "I may be leaving for Greece tomorrow night. You can get hold of me on my cell anytime. Shannon said she'd keep an eye on you while I'm gone."

More like Maggie *told* Shannon. "I don't need a babysitter." When Maggie had been only sixteen, she'd been taking care of two kids. Did she think she was the only one who could do anything?

"Check in with her now and then and let her know how you're doing. Okay?" Maggie said. "Oh, and I rescheduled your orientation at Georgetown for when I get back."

Kate grabbed a mug from the cabinet and poured herself some coffee. "I told you I'm not going."

"Yes, you are. It's important."

"Not to me." Kate turned around, took a deep breath and went for it. "I've decided to take an apprenticeship with Rufus."

Maggie stalled in the act of putting a stack of plates in the cupboard. "What?"

"You heard me." She squared her shoulders. "No Georgetown. At least not right now."

Maggie closed the dishwasher and paced. "So that's it? You want to throw pots?"

She made it sound as if Kate had decided to flip burgers at the greasy spoon down the block. "Have you ever looked at my work?" Kate asked, shaken. "I mean really looked at it?"

"Of course I have."

"You don't like it, do you?"

"Kate, what I think doesn't have anything to do with it. Do you have any idea how hard it is to make a living as an artist?"

"You think I suck."

"That's not true!"

"Well, you're wrong." Kate did her own pacing on the other side of the center island. "Rufus thinks my work is extraordinary. He usually only takes on potters with experience, but he's making an exception for me."

"If he really cared about you, he'd want you to finish college first."

"His intern had to quit early and is going back to Japan right after the exhibit. He needs someone in two weeks. If I don't do this, I don't know when I'll have another opportunity. He's got a waiting list of applicants as long as my arm."

"If you're as talented as he says, there will be just as good an internship available *after* you graduate."

"But probably not with Rufus. Maggie, he's a respected potter. His work is in museums all over the world. The Smithsonian, even!" She stopped and crossed her arms. "This is what I want to do. And you can't make me go to Georgetown."

"You're right I can't." Maggie's jaw worked. She pursed her lips, narrowed her eyes.

Here it came. The consequence. Kate looked away and waited. Two seconds. Three.

"I'm taking your car away," Maggie said.

"You can't do that!"

"Oh, yes I can. Who makes the loan and insurance payments?"

"Argh!" Kate threw her hands up in disgust. "Fine. Take the car. I don't care." She stalked back to her bedroom and slammed the door. God, she was sick of this. Sick of it.

MAGGIE'S MORNING WAS SHOT. Completely. She sat at her desk, returned a few e-mails and phone calls, but she never seemed to accomplish much of anything after arguments with Kate, not to mention the fact that she was on pins and needles hoping to hear back from Giannis on their proposal.

Nick, for his part, looked exhausted. She wasn't sure if it was the dark circles under his eyes, or the khaki shorts and collared knit shirt he'd worn that caused the most damage to his previously polished image. In any case, after grabbing a midmorning snack, he'd destroyed every preconceived notion Maggie had about him by lying down on the couch and falling fast asleep.

"Go home," she'd said when he'd first stood up and yawned. "You can call me when you hear from Giannis."

"No, I still have more reading to do. I'm going to close my eyes for a few minutes."

That had been close to three hours ago, and he was still dead to the world. Maggie and Shannon had been on the phone, in and out, up and down, and still he never awoke.

Watching him now was making Maggie tired. She crossed her office and tilted her head to look at him. It was amazing how a man so intense and serious could look so vulnerable in his sleep, only it wasn't a peaceful slumber, that's for sure.

He'd been tossing and turning, and occasionally emitting low, quiet groans. This was a troubled sleep. She couldn't help wondering what he was dreaming about, could barely keep herself from kneeling beside him and smoothing his brow, curling into him and holding him. Instead, she found a soft fleece pillow and squished it under his head.

With a heavy sigh, Maggie turned around. Some fresh air and something to eat would get her back on track. She poked her head into Shannon's office. "Want to get some lunch?"

Shannon ran a couple invoices through their postage machine. "Ahh, sorry, Mags. I've got plans." She opened a desk drawer, pulled out her purse, and checked her lipstick. Shannon always looked pretty. Today, she almost sparkled.

"Must be someone special."

"Maybe."

"Who're you meeting?"

"None of your business."

Maggie perched on the corner of Shannon's desk.

"Craig, huh?" She was wondering if yesterday afternoon's crisis meeting would kindle old feelings.

"And don't even think about telling me that if I see him," Shannon said, slamming the drawer shut, "you'll take my car away, too."

"Hey!" Maggie shot to her feet, feeling defensive. "That's not fair."

"Threatening Kate isn't fair."

"What am I supposed to do?"

"You guys are way too much alike. That's the problem."

"Except she's screwing up. Big time."

"How do you know?" Shannon stood and slipped into her pale pink suit coat. "One of these days, Maggie, you're going to wake up and realize life's too short for doing everything your way. Sometimes a person's gotta do and not think."

Maggie followed Shannon out to the elevators. "Doing without thinking first only gets people into trouble."

"Keep on telling yourself that, honey, and you won't have much of a life left to worry about."

"What's that supposed to mean?" Maggie asked as they entered the elevator and headed down to the street.

"Figure it out, Maggie."

"What in the world's gotten into you?"

The elevator hit the first floor, and they stepped outside.

"I don't know!" Shannon looked away, frustrated. "Maybe I'm sick of my life the way it is. Maybe I want a few changes. Maybe you could use a few changes, too." Abruptly, she walked away.

A car honked on the street. A stranger nudged Maggie's elbows as he hurried past her. "Enjoy your lunch with Craig!" she yelled before Shannon disappeared around the corner.

Let it go. This was as good a time as any to practice.

"GREAT. PERFECT. WE'LL BE THERE, GIANNIS. *Andeeo*," Nick said, hoping he sounded relatively coherent.

Still groggy from sleep, he snapped his cell phone closed and fumbled to set it on the coffee table. From his prone position on the office couch, he looked around for Maggie. She must've gone out. He glanced at the clock. Hell, he'd been sleeping for hours. He rubbed his hands over his face and stared at the ceiling. An intense sense of relief settled over him. In two days, he'd be in Greece. Years of waiting, planning and anticipating would soon be over.

Then he could get on with his life.

He stretched, went into Shannon's office, poured himself a cup of coffee and considered the contents of their minifridge. Yogurt and grapes. Not much of a meal by his standards, but he wasn't really hungry.

By the time Maggie got back from what he'd presumed was lunch, he was wide awake and back in his chair finishing the last of the reading material she'd laid out for him at the beginning of the week.

"Howdy." She breezed in and set a sub sandwich in front of him. "Hungry?"

"No, thanks."

"Where's Shannon?"

"I have no idea."

"She didn't come back from lunch? Weird." She dropped her purse, a backpack type clunky thing on her desk. "How are you coming with all that reading?"

"Done. Finished. *Epeeteloos*." He set the last document in the pile.

"In that case." She reached for a drawer in the credenza behind her.

"Stop right there. I've read enough." Granted, this

business was complicated, but he was as prepared as he was ever going to get. "If you pull out one more contract, manual or code book, I won't be responsible for what happens next." He wouldn't strangle her, but he might kiss her senseless.

"Alrighty then." She raised her eyebrows at him and managed to look both comical and cute at the same time.

After spending several days crammed together in her office, the initial antagonism of their relationship had morphed into quiet acceptance, if not respect. In fact, he'd probably hire her to work for him any day, and that was saying a lot.

"Besides, it's Friday." He glanced at his watch. "Four o'clock. And I just got off the phone with Giannis."

"You did?" That got her attention. "What'd he say?"

"We got the contract."

"Really?"

"Really."

"Yesss!" She jumped up and down like a kid, acted as if she might come and hug him and stopped, completely unsure what to do with herself. She laughed, and he couldn't help smiling. "Thank you."

That, he hadn't expected. "I didn't do much. Like I said in the beginning. A little testosterone and you had it bagged."

"You tipped the scales, and this is a big contract. We have to celebrate." She opened the door to her apartment, ran up the steps, and yelled, "I'll be right back down."

He waited. And waited. No, he shouldn't join her in her apartment. *Ah, hell, screw shouldn'ts.* He climbed the steps two at a time and found her pulling a bottle of champagne out of the top shelf in the refrigerator. She spun around, and her smile faltered when she saw him in her apartment. He was stepping out of bounds and he didn't care.

"I'm sick of that office."

"Me, too." She grinned and grabbed two flute glasses.

While she uncorked the bottle, he absorbed the feel of her apartment. If he'd imagined her living space, this would've been it. Though the rooms were relatively small, they were packed with life. He could've sat here for days looking around. Every wall was painted a different color; there was lime-green, burgundy, burnt orange, hot pink. Light streamed full blast through the unshuttered windows. Bookshelves lined two entire walls in the main living area, and pottery was everywhere. On tabletops, counters, and shelves.

"You've got an interesting place here."

"Kate's the artistic one. She paints and decorates. I clutter."

He reached down and ran his fingers over an oddly shaped platter on the coffee table. The glaze was a fascinating amalgamation of mat black and shiny gold. "Did Kate make this?"

Maggie's smile brightened. "Yep. Her stuff's all over the place."

"She's very talented."

"I know. Look at these." She pulled him over to a glass-enclosed curio case by the far wall. "She went through a game phase in eighth grade." A set of jacks, dice, a child's top sat on the shelf.

"They look made from metal. Are they clay?"

Maggie nodded and showed him a shelf of teapots, some fanciful and creative, and others truly perfect in form and function. "I don't know how she does it."

"Amazing."

"All of Kate's teachers have fawned over her work, and she won first place at an art fair earlier this summer." Maggie went back to the counter to pour champagne into two flutes. Suddenly, her smile disappeared, her excitement fizzled.

"But?" Nick prompted.

"No matter how good she is, I don't know how she'll pay her rent, let alone feed herself."

"She'll never know unless she tries." He had the feeling Kate shared Maggie's strength of mind. Like her older sister, Kate could probably accomplish anything.

"I don't want to talk about that anymore." Maggie handed him a glass before raising her own. "To Greece."

"Opa!" He clinked his glass with hers, and watched her over the rim as he gulped down half the bubbly.

"Okay." She refilled both their glasses. "So you think you know all you need to know about programming, eh?"

"Quiz me."

"That, I can't resist." She set the bottle down and climbed onto a bar stool at the island in her kitchen. "What's source code? What's object-oriented programming? What operating system does the Greek government use?" She threw one question on top of another after him. "If we get the contract, how long will the project take? How many programmers will be focusing their efforts on this job?"

One after another, he effortlessly answered everything she threw at him. As he did so, he couldn't stop thinking about how her lips looked as she talked, smooth, wet, glistening with champagne. How would she feel? Her skin, warm and soft? Her hair, coarse or silky?

To hell with waiting until after his business in Greece

was settled. It'd been three and half years since he'd felt the intimate touch of a woman. Three and a half years. As long as he chose the right woman, no harm, no foul. Maggie was a big girl. He'd make the situation clear to her. No commitments. She probably wouldn't be close to heartbroken if he ended up dead or in a Greek jail by this time next week.

"What is a—"

"Enough, Maggie," he said, slowly closing the distance between them. "I told you. I'm ready."

"Okay." She sighed.

"You sound disappointed."

"Maybe a little." She took another sip. "You catch on a lot quicker than I do."

"I don't know about that."

"Believe it or not, this is difficult for me. I'm not used to relying on anyone else to reach my business goals."

Tough cookie crumbles. The sudden show of vulnerability touched him. "I'm sorry if I've made this harder for you."

"I'm fine." She shrugged her shoulders, refitted her armor. "You're ready for Athens."

And he was ready for her. Now. "Are you seeing anyone?" he asked.

"What?" Her lips parted suggestively.

"Are you in a relationship with a man?"

"I think our training session is over." She stood and pushed her stool back in place.

"Maggie, it's a simple question."

"Not that it's any of your business, but no." She went to the kitchen counter. "I don't have time for relationships, and most men can't handle being second in a woman's life."

"I have no problem with that."

"I didn't ask if you did."

"Do you hate all men, or just me?"

"I don't hate you." Her head snapped up. "You—"

"Drive you crazy?"

"Yes!"

He grinned and walked toward her.

"No! I mean…not in that way."

"Push your buttons?"

"Yes—no!" She laughed nervously.

He took the champagne flute from her hand and set their glasses down on the counter. Momentarily, his attention was arrested by one of the photographs on the wall of Maggie, quite a few years younger, with her sisters and an attractive older woman, probably their mother, at an oceanside resort. He ignored it, not wanting to think about her personal life, that she might have a personal life. This was about physical recreation. Sex. No ties. No tomorrows. He could promise no more than that. "I'm not good at games, Maggie," he said. "But I'm pretty sure you want me as much as I want you."

Rich flecks of gold sparked in her eyes, confirming his assessment. "And you have an overinflated ego."

He'd hoped for no pretense, but if it was cat-and-mouse she wanted, he'd do his best to accommodate. "Probably. That doesn't change anything," he whispered. "We're not children." Leaning one hand against the countertop, his chest nearly brushed against her shoulder. "As long as we're responsible and careful, there's nothing wrong with indulging our bodies. Sex is as natural as rain."

She backed away. "It would also end our business arrangement."

"Not if we keep things simple. Nothing serious. No

commitments. We're both adults. You're letting one insignificant detail get in the way."

"Insignif—"

"Shh." He touched his finger to her lips, exactly where he wanted to put his mouth. "The moment I stepped into your office." *God, was it less than a week ago?* "The moment we first met, I reacted to you. I've been reacting for the past week. I'm reacting now. Let it go, Maggie."

"People have been telling me that a lot lately."

He reached for her hand, brought the inside of her wrist to his mouth. The butterfly. So beautiful against her pale skin. Her pulse was racing. He glanced back to her face, her lips, parted and wet. It had been far too long since he'd kissed a woman, and this woman made him want again.

She closed her eyes, a silent invitation, and he leaned in, lightly pressing his mouth to hers. So soft, warm. Her breath shuddered against him. Their tongues collided and she moaned.

He groaned back and brought her closer. Three years without a woman, or not, she tasted so very, very good.

She fell back in his arms, as if her knees had given way, then, as if rousing from a trance, she stiffened and moved away. "I can't believe it." Her chest rose and fell with short bursts of air. "For God's sake! You're married!"

Stunned, Nick stepped back. Not that he'd tried keeping his marriage a secret, but how would she know about Kyrena? "Maggie, you don't underst—"

"Oh, I understand all right," she interrupted, clearly infuriated. She backed farther away, putting the center island between them. "This is where you tell me your wife's a bitch, or that she doesn't know how to satisfy you in bed. That if you'd known about me, you never would have gotten married. That you don't usually do this kind of thing. The attraction was overwhelming." She glared at him as if he were no better than a slithering snake, the lowest of the low. "Doesn't the commitment of marriage mean anything to you?"

The words hit him like a hammer between the eyes. For three and a half years he'd kept his vows, honoring his promise. During that time, he'd never slept with Kyrena, let alone any other women, wanting nothing more out of their arrangement than to know Kyrena was safe, only to be accused of being an adulterer *after* his divorce.

Maggie had no right to judge him, let alone judge him falsely and harshly. Now, for all he cared, she could go right on thinking she had all the answers. Maybe next time she'd either do a more thorough investigation, or stay out of people's personal lives altogether.

"You have two children," she continued. "Maybe you can betray them. I won't."

"Enough!" he yelled. Her self-righteousness made his stomach roil, but he'd be damned before he'd set the record straight. For all he cared, she could stew in her own heat. "I know what I felt in that kiss, Maggie." He strode toward the door. "This is far from over."

CHAPTER EIGHT

SO MUCH FOR NICK BEING *safe!*

Maggie couldn't believe what had happened. Startled, almost as much by her own reaction as by Nick's forwardness, she stood motionless listening to the sound of his footfalls pounding down her apartment stairs. She listened at the stairwell, and only when their outer foyer door closed with resounding force did she allow herself to relax.

What an ass. Who did he think he was? Of all the sleezy, arrogant...

Ah, hell. She had to be honest with herself. He wasn't the only one at fault. She'd been an idiot. She swallowed her anger. He was absolutely right. She *did* want him, had spent almost every second of every hour of the past five days wanting him. That was the problem.

She hadn't expected to feel this way, but it was heaven having a man nearby this week. To deny that she'd been consumed with thoughts of touching him, holding him, kissing him would be an outright lie. The inside of her wrist, her tattoo, burned where he'd kissed her. Where his warm breath had touched her the hair stood on end.

Briskly, she rubbed the sensations away. For the life of her, she couldn't understand what it was about him she found so damned irresistible. Oh, he was handsome in a dark, enigmatic sort of way, and she had been immensely impressed by how quickly he'd caught on to the intricacies of this industry, but she'd always preferred men she could direct, men who wouldn't interfere with her plans, her life. Her control.

So what kind of man was Nick Ballos?

Maggie had known him less than a week, but she'd spent enough time with him to know he was certainly not a typical philandering flirt. He paid no attention whatsoever to Shannon, who was ten times prettier than Maggie, and at the Walker party, where women were falling all over themselves wanting his attention, he'd acted as if he couldn't get out of there fast enough. None of it made sense.

Shannon. Her sister would help her sort through everything. Maggie ran outside, and, ten minutes and twelve blocks later, she was knocking on her sister's apartment door.

"Maggie." Shannon, her hair mussed, was dressed in her pale pink bathrobe. "What are you doing here?"

"I need to talk." Maggie marched in as she'd done a hundred times since Shannon had gotten her own apartment only a few months ago and threw her purse on the sofa. "You didn't come back from lunch. What's up?"

She glanced at her watch. It was only six, and Shannon looked as if she'd spent the last several hours in bed—

Ah, oh. Craig Stanton? Maybe. Probably. Oh, boy.

"This was a bad idea." Shaking her head, Maggie kept her gaze firmly averted from the bedroom as she headed out the door. "I guess I haven't gotten used to you living your own life." She stopped in the hall and turned around. "Sorry, Shannon."

"Maggie, come back."

"I'll call you in the morning," she said over her shoulder.

"Maggie!" Shannon grabbed her hand.

"My timing sucks."

"You wouldn't be here if it wasn't important."

She hesitated.

"You'll make me feel like more of a jerk if you leave."

Her sister's plea and pathetically apologetic expression were all the encouragement she needed. Once Maggie was inside the apartment, she stood awkwardly in the doorway, not sure what to do or say, how to act. She couldn't be Shannon's caretaker anymore, so what was Maggie to Shannon? For the first time ever, Maggie felt as if she were an outsider in Shannon's life.

And rightly so. Her sister did have a life, separate from their family. It was about time she created that space Shannon so needed. "I should go."

"Maggie, sit down. There's something I have to tell you anyway."

Maggie dropped onto the sofa and clasped her hands between her knees. Shannon had done such a nice job decorating. While the apartment was far too clean and contemporary for Maggie's taste, it fit Shannon.

"Want a drink?" Shannon asked.

"No, thanks." Maggie stood and paced in front of the windows, her impatience building.

"Ah, come on, Mags." A man's voice sounded from behind her. "At least join us in a toast."

Maggie whirled around. It was Craig, but the sight of him here was still a bit of a shocker. "Hey."

"Don't look so surprised," Shannon said. "You had to know this was coming."

These two belonged together. "All I can say is, follow through with a wedding this time, okay?"

Shannon set the champagne bottle on the slate counter and grabbed Craig's hand, bringing it to her lips. "We already did," she said, her clear, forceful voice nearly breaking, her eyes locked on Craig's face.

"You got married? Today?" Maggie hadn't been aware of any expectations she'd had regarding her sisters' weddings, but this somehow didn't fit the bill.

Shannon dropped Craig's hand. "Maggie, don't be upset. Please."

"It's not that we didn't want you and Kate with us," Craig said. "It's that…my family, my mom…we'll have a party later. Shannon and I didn't want any fuss right now."

"I get it," Maggie said, standing. "I really do. It's just that…everything's so out of control. You. Kate. I don't know what I'm doing. What I'm supposed to do."

"Let us live our lives?"

Much, much easier said than done.

Except in this case. Maggie smiled at Shannon. "I'm very happy for you both."

Craig popped the cork out of the champagne bottle and poured three glasses.

"Congratulations!" Maggie hugged them each in turn and then downed the champagne.

"Whoa! That was fast," Shannon said. "What's going on?"

Maggie set her empty class on the counter and studied Craig. "Maybe it's a good thing you're here. You've known Nick for a long time, right?"

"Yeah." Craig set down his own glass.

"Well, I need to know—I don't understand—"

"She's falling in love with him," Shannon offered, matter-of-factly.

"Good," Craig said. "Nick could use a woman like you in his life."

Shannon looked stricken, and Maggie couldn't keep from laughing. "Marriage vows have suddenly taken on a whole new meaning, huh, Shannon?"

"What did I say?" Craig looked back and forth between them.

"He's married," Maggie said. "Has two kids. I've seen the whole crew in the parking lot outside my office window."

"When?" Craig asked.

"A day or two after Nick signed on with us."

"Well, all I can say is that things aren't always what they seem." Craig poured himself another glass of champagne. "Have you asked Nick what's going on?"

"So you're going to pull the whole client confidentiality thing on me?" Maggie headed for the door. "Pretend I didn't come here."

"Craig," Shannon said, the warning tone clear.

"Wait." Craig stopped Maggie with a tug on her arm.

"The crazy thing is," Maggie said, "he looked as if he were in love with his wife, adored his kids. I don't get why he's interested in an affair—"

"The kids aren't his."

"What?"

Craig took a deep breath. "Kyrena was married to Nick's best friend, Yanni Kythos. A short while after Yanni was killed, Kyrena's brother-in-law filed child endangerment charges against her in an attempt to get custody of Yanni's kids. What he was really after was

Kyrena. Years earlier, the brothers had a falling-out over her. Stephano was obsessed."

Maggie stared out the window, processing what he'd said. Strangely enough, the pieces fit. "So Nick brought her to the U.S. and married her."

"Purely out of a sense of duty, and if you know Nick at all—"

"He would do something exactly like that," Maggie finished for him. "But I know what I saw. They're in love."

"You're positive?" Craig cocked his head. "Then maybe you can explain to me why Kyrena just moved to California and married her bodyguard."

"What the hell is going on?" Shannon asked.

"He's divorced," Craig said. "Signed the papers last week."

Maggie shook her head. "I saw—"

"What you saw might have been love, all right. The kind of love between family members. Nick has known Kyrena since they were kids. He'd do anything for her. Except sleep with her." Craig's eyes softened. "Once she was safe and she had her green card, his job was done. It was never a real marriage, Maggie. Never."

I KNOW WHAT I FELT IN THAT KISS, Maggie. This is far from over. That's what Nick had said, purposefully letting Maggie think he was still married. Well, maybe she'd jumped to conclusions, but she sure as hell didn't deserve to be punished for it.

With adrenaline fueling her anger, Maggie followed Craig's directions. She turned onto the drive to Nick's house, parked in front of a massive, two-story home, and marched up the front steps. When no one answered the door after several rings, she stepped back and glanced across the front facade looking for any sign of life inside the imposing structure. Although the house was completely dark, he had to be here.

Through the warm summer air, she marched across the lawn and around the corner of the house. Twilight was settling, turning everything dark and creating shadows. Damn. This place had to cost a fortune. Pool. Perfectly landscaped yard.

A faint ray of light shone through the dense woods highlighting a sidewalk through the bushes. As she followed the path, a light breeze ruffled the leaves on the tall trees and the shape of a small guest or carriage house took form. Several lights twinkled and there was movement behind the blinds. That had to be where Nick lived. Kyrena must've lived in the main house with the kids.

Suddenly her feet felt heavy, weighted, as if she'd stepped in cement. Crickets chirped from the nearby bushes, an owl hooted off in the distance, and her rage evaporated as quickly as it had formed. She stopped short of the door as reality hit. She had no claims on Nick and no right to be here. If she knocked on that door, she'd only make a fool of herself. She turned around as the front door opened.

Dressed only in a pair of shorts, Nick stood a few heart-stopping feet away. She felt her gaze immediately drawn to the series of small scars dotting the right side of his chest, felt her fingers itching to reach out and explore.

"Hello, Maggie." He snapped his cell phone shut and crossed his arms. "Craig told me you'd be looking for me."

She stared at his wet, disheveled black hair, at the droplets of water beading on his shoulders and upper arms. It was painfully obvious that only a moment ago he'd been in a shower. Naked. Soapy. Her breath caught.

"Hey!" He reached for her arms. "You okay?"

"No. Definitely not okay." The tangy scent of his shampoo swirled around her. His breath fanned her cheek. He was too close. She placed her hands flat against him thinking she'd create some distance. Mistake. The feel of his damp skin beneath her fingers only heightened every other sensation. "You lied to me," she whispered.

"I never lied about anything."

"Oohh!" she breathed out in frustration and pushed against him, breaking his hold. "You didn't tell me that your marriage hadn't been real, let alone that you were divorced. I'd call that lying."

"That was a deliberate omission and a well-deserved one, at that. You can come in and talk about it, or stand outside, your choice. Either way, I'm going inside to grab a towel and finish drying off." He walked away, leaving the front door wide open.

She should go. Now. What was she doing here, anyway?

"Cold feet again, Maggie?" He looked over his shoulder. "Does that happen a lot?"

Dammit, she needed to hear the truth from him. She stepped over the threshold and closed the door behind her.

The kitchen, dining and sitting areas of Nick's home were all combined in one large area. Muted colors of greens and rusts created a welcome, earthy feel. Soft light emanated from several lamps around the room and a large-screen TV hung on one wall along with a bit of artwork, here and there, but the main focal point was a fieldstone fireplace flanked by large windows overlooking heavy woods.

His home looked lived-in, relaxed, comfortable, not at all what she'd expected from this always immaculately dressed man. There were a few dirty dishes in the sink, papers and mail on the countertop. His shoes and socks sat next to a chair and magazines and books were strewn across the coffee table.

Suddenly, Maggie's bones felt as if they were melting, her muscles fatigued. She wanted to curl up on his overstuffed couch and sleep for a week.

"Go ahead. Sit down." Nick motioned toward the sitting area before walking in the opposite direction down the hall. "I'll be right back."

Maggie had only taken a few tentative steps before he returned wearing a white T-shirt and rubbing a bath towel over his head. A clean soapy scent drifted toward her, and it took it every ounce of willpower she possessed not to walk right up to him and run her hands across his chest.

He stopped at the table in the kitchen and, draping the towel around his neck, finished off what was left in a glass that had been sitting on the counter. He plunked several more chunks of ice into the short tumbler. "Drink?"

"No."

He poured out a small shot of whiskey, swirled it around and downed it in one gulp. "Okay. What do you want to know?"

"Was it really a green card marriage?"

"Yes."

"Did Kyrena and the children live with you here, or—"

"They lived in the main house. Proximity was necessary to maintain the pretense for the Department of Immigration. After starting off under one roof, though, it didn't take long to figure out she and the kids needed their own space."

"You were married and you never slept together?"

"Never."

Maggie own insecurities flared. She'd felt the heat in Nick's kisses, so how was it that a man with such potent desires wanted Maggie and not Kyrena? "Did you ever want to sleep with her?"

He laughed. "Maybe when I was sixteen and my hormones were telling me that any body with breasts would suffice."

"She was much more than that. I saw her."

"When?"

"Her limo came to the parking lot across from my office."

"Ahh." He nodded.

"She's a beautiful woman."

"Who never noticed any man but Yanni. Until Carlos."

"You love her." She held her breath.

"Yes." He studied her reaction. "Like a sister."

Her relief was palpable, and, abruptly, he turned away. His profile looked cold and distant as if he were sending notice to the world to stay away. Now Maggie knew it was nothing more than a facade, a wall built around him to keep her out. No one could give so many years of his life for another person and be as uncaring as he wanted the world to believe.

"And now?" she asked.

"Now Kyrena and the children have their citizenship. That's all that matters."

"Is it?" She wanted to reach out and hold him, such a tough guy. She thought of how vulnerable he'd looked sleeping on her office couch, how troubled.

"And Nick? He doesn't matter? Is that what Kyrena would say?"

"You don't know Kyrena. Don't pretend to know what she'd think."

"I saw the devotion in her eyes. That counts for something. What you did for her—"

"Was no different than what any good friend would do for another." He reeled around. "Who'd you get all this devotion crap from? Stanton?"

"Why didn't you explain to me the real reason behind your marriage?"

"Oh, that's rich, Maggie." Nick laughed. "Does this question ring a bell? *Doesn't the commitment of marriage mean anything to you?* Or how 'bout this one? *Maybe you can betray your children, I can't.*"

The memory of those words hit her like a splash of cold water in the face.

"You wouldn't have believed me if I'd told you the truth," he said. "If I'd tried to explain I was in a green card marriage, that I'd divorced *just last week*, you'd have laughed in my face."

"I was wrong. I misjudged you. I'm sorry."

"Apology accepted." He set his empty glass down on the counter and headed for the door. "Now you'd better go."

Maggie walked toward him, feeling as if someone else, a different woman, had taken over her body. For so long, she'd focused on taking care of Shannon and Kate, her business. There'd never been a man who made her want anything different. Until this one. She stopped in front of him and tentatively traced the outline of his lips with her fingertips.

"I don't want to leave."

CHAPTER NINE

PLEASURE AND PAIN, HEAVEN AND HELL.

It had been a mistake not turning Maggie away the moment Nick had found her at his door. He'd known in some remote part of his brain what might happen if he invited her inside his home. Still, he hadn't been able to stop himself.

He studied her. Head tilted back as she gazed at him. Lips slightly parted. The green of her eyes bright and warm with need, oh, God, for him.

And his guard nearly collapsed. He wanted to be angry with her for her swift condemnation of him back at her apartment, wanted to despise her quirky mixture of determination, self-righteousness, and vulnerability, but her apology, so simple and uncomplicated, had disarmed him. Two steps and he could lift her into his arms and finish what he'd started earlier tonight in her apartment.

And then what? He closed his eyes against the sight of her. Making love to her would only pull her down alongside him into the hellhole of revenge he'd been living in for almost five years. She didn't deserve that. "I changed my mind." He looked at her again. "I had an urge back at your apartment, and you were available."

"Why do you want to hurt me? What did I ever do to

you?" Then her eyes cleared, and she shook her head. "You're lying. Pushing me away. Why?"

Tomorrow night they'd be heading to Athens. He'd be focused on finding Tarik and the man who hired him, and she'd be busting her gorgeous ass for another software contract. He had to be honest with himself; a few tumbles with Maggie would never be enough, and a few tumbles was all he had time for. Once he got to Greece he could not afford to be distracted, by anything, or anyone.

"Maggie, I made a promise." Nick held her away from him. "A long time ago. Until I resolve some things, my life's not really my own." He opened the door and stepped back for her to leave. "Let it go. Leave. Now." *While I can still let you go.*

"No." She stepped closer, bumped the door closed with her hip, and snuck her hands under his T-shirt, across his skin, into the tufts of hair on his chest. Though her touch was gentle, this petite bundle of woman held the power to conquer him, change his course. He couldn't let that happen.

"Maggie, stop." He pulled her hands away from his suddenly overly sensitive skin. She looked into his eyes. And smiled. Lifting up his shirt, she bent forward, kissed his chest, lashing at his nipple with her tongue. He wasn't kidding anyone. She was already well aware of her power, and the heat he'd felt before paled in comparison to this explosion. "Don't." He held her away.

"Why?" Her eyes almost pleaded with him. "There's nothing to stop us." Her mouth opened, waiting for him.

What would it be like to feel her lips, not in the whisper-soft touch they'd shared, but a real kiss, crashing through them both? Once. One real kiss.

Before stopping to think, he drew her into his arms

and their mouths met with a fury of sensation. Warm. Wet. He brought his lips to hers, again and again, making up for every other time he'd wanted this and had denied himself the pleasure. She was his for a moment. He intended on making the most of it. He buried his hands in her hair, held her neck, her breasts.

Her fingers dipped beneath the waistband of his shorts. He must be a masochist, reveling in her touch, in the rush, the feel of her breasts crushed against him, the pressure of her hands. She owned him, and he didn't care.

Two layers of fabric was too frustrating to ignore. He slipped his hand beneath her T-shirt, grazing the smooth, taut surface of her belly and pushed off her bra. When he cupped her breast, her answering whimper shattered what was left of his restraint.

One more indulgence, that was it. To feel her bare skin against him. He pulled her T-shirt over her head, revealing a line of tattoos along her left side, small multicolored butterflies running from under her arm all the way to her hip. The black mixed with bright colors looked lovely against her pale skin. "That is so sexy," he said, surprising himself.

"You? Like tats?"

"I do on you." He unsnapped her bra, then held her close to him, burying his face in the thick curls at the nape of her neck, breathing in her scent, holding her hips against him. This wasn't nearly enough. He cradled her face, made her look into his eyes. "I can't make any promises, Maggie, about a future together. You need to know that."

"I'm not asking for any," she whispered into the palm of his hand. "A few nights. That's all."

"We have tonight. One night. Once I'm in Athens, you can't be involved with me. Can you deal with that?"

She felt herself melting again, falling into him. She no longer *needed* Nick Ballos. She *wanted* him. For the first time in her life, she wanted a man. "I can deal with anything as long as it involves you, me and a bed—"

The heavy beat of Kate's latest favorite song sounded from Maggie's purse. *Shit.* "That's my phone," Maggie said, backing away from him so she could think.

"Ignore it."

"I can't. That's Kate's ring tone." It was almost midnight. "She wouldn't be calling unless it's important." Maggie reached into her purse and flipped open her cell phone. "Kate, what's going on?"

"This is Officer Patecki with the D.C. police department. Is this Maggie Dillon?"

"This is Maggie. What happened? What's wrong?"

"Are you Kate Dillon's guardian?"

"Is she all right?"

Nick pulled on his T-shirt.

"Yes, ma'am, she's fine. Maybe too fine. We busted the party she was at and Kate blew a point one one."

"She's been drinking?"

"A lot. The legal limit for driving is point zero seven. Good thing she wasn't behind the wheel, or she'd be in much more serious trouble. Can you come and get her?"

Now, Maggie was pissed. "Can she sleep it off in jail?"

The officer didn't say anything.

"I'm sorry. I'm angry," Maggie said. "Where is she?"

The officer gave Maggie the address. As she snatched her purse, her hands shook.

Nick reached out. "I'll drive you."

Close to an hour later, he slowed down in front of Kate's friend's house. Three squad cars and a slew of personal vehicles were parked in the driveway or on the street outside the house. "Over there." She pointed to the first available space and jumped out of the car.

"I'm here for Kate Dillon," Maggie said to the officer at the door.

A buzz-cut young cop looked her up and down, took in her tattoo and ear piercings. "Parents were supposed to come."

Maggie got this all the time. Tonight she wasn't feeling particularly patient. "Our parents are dead," she said. His stern expression didn't soften one iota. "I'm Kate Dillon's guardian."

"Maybe if you set a better example, this kid wouldn't be in so much trouble."

Screw you. She had to admit she'd been feeling that way the entire drive over here.

"Hey," Nick said to the officer. "That wasn't necessary."

The patrolman snapped his head to the side. "Go on in."

Maggie wrapped Nick's sweatshirt more tightly around her, went through the front door, and found a dozen or so kids scattered throughout the house. Some occupied chairs. Most sat collapsed on a floor littered with shot glasses, empty bottles of cheap booze and plastic cups. Many of the girls had been or still were crying, mascara smudged around their eyes and streaking down their cheeks. The boys looked shell-shocked. Unfortunately, Maggie recognized many of the kids. Most of them had been in the Dillon apartment at one time or another, eaten pizza, watched movies, hung out.

Kate stood in the kitchen and paced back and forth. "I don't get why you cops had to come here," she said to an officer standing nearby. "We weren't bothering anyone."

"That's not the way the next door neighbor saw it."

"Who was it? I wanna know."

"Kate," Maggie said.

She turned, and a resigned expression passed over Kate's features before she set her jaw. "Oh, this is just great."

"Let's go."

"I don't wanna go with you."

"You don't have a choice."

"Yes, I do." She turned to the cop. "I don't have to go with her, do I?"

"Are you her guardian?" the officer asked Maggie. He sounded like the man who'd called her cell.

Maggie nodded.

He turned back to Kate. "You can either go with your sister, or you can go to jail. Which one is it?"

Kate scowled and flicked her chin toward Nick. "What's he doing here?"

"He drove me."

"Perfect." She stalked off toward the door.

Maggie was about to follow Kate when the cop stopped her with a hand on her arm. "You got a minute?"

"Go with Kate, please," she asked Nick and glanced back at the cop. "You gonna chew me out, too?"

"No." He was quite a bit older than the little shit cop at the front door. "Have you been in charge of her for a while?"

Maggie nodded and braced herself for the criticism sure to come. "Ten years."

"Really." He raised his eyebrows, assessing her age. "Well, you must be doing something right."

Tears came out of nowhere, welling in her eyes. "At this particular moment, it feels as if I've done everything wrong."

The cop sighed and crossed his arms. "Not to make

light of the situation, but we see a lot of this during the high school years. For several of these kids, tonight's the second or third offense. This is her first. You can't be doing everything wrong."

"No. It probably means she hasn't been caught all the other times."

"She claims this is a first, and I think I believe her."

Maggie sniffled and dried her cheeks. "You do?"

He nodded. "And she graduated, didn't she?"

"Yeah. With good enough grades to get accepted at Georgetown."

"Well, there you go. Your sister was respectful tonight, but she stood up for herself. While that's not all bad, I'm guessing she's quite a handful."

Maggie chuckled.

"Put a cork in this, and she'll be all right."

Maggie bit the inside of her cheek to keep from breaking down in tears again. "Thanks."

"I told her if I see her again," he said with a wink. "I'll skip the call and throw her right in jail."

Ten minutes later, Nick was driving Maggie and Kate back to their apartment. Maggie could've cut the tension in the car with dental floss. Finally, she couldn't stand it. She turned around and pinned Kate to the backseat with one look. "You are so grounded!"

Kate glared back. "You can't ground me! I'm seventeen years old!"

Oh, crap. Maggie hadn't grounded Kate since her sister had been about twelve. How did real parents go about keeping an almost adult in lockdown? She was so in over her head. "I can sell your car, take your money. Is that what you want?"

"Empty threats!"

Maggie took a deep breath and started counting to ten. She only made it to three. "You—" she jabbed a finger toward Kate "—are so going with me to Greece!"

CHAPTER TEN

On the flight to Greece, Maggie sat between Nick and Kate, but she may as well have been sitting between two deaf-mutes for all the interaction they offered.

Kate had started with the silent treatment the moment she realized nothing could be said or done to get Maggie to back down on bringing Kate along, so on the thirteen-plus hour flight, when Kate hadn't been sleeping, she'd been pouting. From the looks of it, she planned on maintaining the attitude indefinitely.

As for Nick, although they'd all slept a good share of the flight, Maggie couldn't help noticing that the closer they got to Athens, the more withdrawn he'd become. It started with her having to ask him the same question two, three times. His eyebrows had drawn together and his mouth had turned down into a perpetual scowl. He didn't eat, drank only water. He spoke with her only when necessary.

Ultimately, she'd given up attempting any conversation and had left him staring silently out of the window into the dark night. By the time they'd arrived in Athens, Nick had turned into a stranger.

Maggie occupied herself on the flight by studying a Greek travel guide and familiarizing herself with some of the customs and language. She'd by no means become an expert, but felt comfortable with her cursory knowledge of Athens, the southern coast and a few of the major islands.

After clearing the airport, they found a cab. Their driver took care of the luggage while Nick opened the back door of the taxi for Maggie and Kate. He climbed into the front seat and told the driver, "The Pláka district, *parakalo*."

Following Nick's advice, Maggie had leased, on very short notice, quite possibly the last available furnished flats downtown near Sýndagma Square and the government buildings. For extended stays, the option was cheaper and would probably be more comfortable than hotel rooms. They could prepare some of their own meals and, if necessary, get some group work done in the evenings.

As they drove, Maggie caught herself rubbernecking her way through Athens. Other than a few spring breaks down in Mexico with her sisters, she hadn't traveled out of the U.S. Even Kate, though plugged into her iPod, was having a hard time keeping her head down.

The young men and women of Athens didn't look all that different from Americans with their trendy clothing and funky hairstyles. The old people, on the other hand, made it seem as if their taxi had driven back in time. The men sat in groups at sidewalk cafés, wearing caps on their heads and old-fashioned glasses, reading newspapers and sipping coffees out of white espresso cups. The old women wore plain dresses and sturdy, no-nonsense shoes with drab black or brown shawls around their shoulders and matching scarves on their heads.

Athens itself, hazy pollution included, probably wasn't much different than most big cities. Well, except for the relentlessly blue sky, the ancient ruins towering in the hilltops and nestled pretty much around any given corner, the sidewalk cafés, open air markets, intricate architectural details, and towering palm trees on the street corners.

Maggie glanced at Nick and wondered at his apparent indifference toward his childhood home. He hadn't said a word to either her or Kate since customs, until he tapped Kate's arms and pointed. "The Acropolis."

"What is it?" Kate asked.

"The highest point of the ancient city."

"Why did they build way up there?"

He was drawing Kate out. Maggie sat back, content to listen.

"It's easy to defend," he explained, "from all sides. But the buildings, like the Temple of Athena, and especially the Parthenon, were intended as a statement to the world, a declaration of power and wealth."

Kate smiled. "It is pretty here."

With the sun beating down and temperatures in the mid-eighties, Maggie felt like she was baking inside the cab. She rolled down her window to get some air moving and took a deep breath. Exhaust on one corner, fried chicken on another and the lemony scent of grilled peppers on yet another. "Where did you live while you were growing up?" she asked Nick.

"Glyfada," he answered with little emotion. "It's a coastal town southeast of here. My father worked in the city, but my mother wanted to be by the ocean."

He was so preoccupied, Maggie couldn't guess what was going on in his mind. "Are you glad to be back after all that time away?"

"There's nothing here for me." He glanced around as they zipped past quaint side streets, old homes, tourist shops and cafés. "Not any longer."

Why not? And if he truly was ambivalent, why had he been so impatient to get back here? It didn't make any sense to Maggie.

The taxi stopped in front of a relatively generic apartment building with balconies overlooking a tree-lined street. Their driver hopped out, setting their luggage at the curb. Maggie paid him. *"Efkhareesto,"* she said, testing out her rudimentary knowledge of Greek. After the cab drove away, she asked Nick, "Did I say that right?"

He corrected her pronunciation and taught her several more key phrases. Kate joined in the impromptu lesson until they located their two flats situated across the hall from each other on the second floor.

The plan was for Kate and Maggie to stay in the smaller two-bedroom apartment, not that Maggie would feel as if she had another person living with her, given Kate's sullen mood. Nick was stuck with the A-Team, who had all arrived together on a previous flight, in the larger four-bedroom. He'd tried finding his own place, but there was nothing suitable available in the area for a few more weeks.

Maggie unlocked hers and Kate's door, and Nick helped them carry in their luggage. Air-conditioned and decorated in crisp, clean blues and whites, the rooms were a cool and comfortable contrast to the outside heat. The furniture was serviceable, and there was a large balcony with an elaborately decorated black metal rail facing the street.

"We have a few hours before Giannis's dinner party," Nick said. "He invited all of us, but if you two would rather do some sightseeing or rest up for tomorrow—"

"No, I think I should go." Maggie was anxious to get the ball rolling on her project. She glanced at Kate.

"Don't look at me." Kate glared back. "I'm not going anywhere with you." She dragged her suitcase down to one of the bedrooms and slammed the door, leaving Nick and Maggie standing in the combined kitchen and living area.

"This is going to be a fun week," Maggie said.

"You did the right thing." It was the first time he'd looked at her, really looked into her eyes since last night, since they'd almost made love. Amazing, how so much could change in a day.

"Did I?"

"She'll get over it."

"What about us?" Maggie asked. "What do we do now?" She knew it was nuts, but she wanted to move toward him, feel his arms around her.

"No tomorrows, Maggie, remember?"

"We didn't even have a today."

"That's probably a good thing."

And he was probably right. Maggie had thought Nick was safe when she'd thought he was married, safe to let in, safe to get close to. This man was so far from safe, it wasn't funny. She'd let herself become friends with him, and here he was now, she had to admit, standing in front of her, quite possibly more dangerous to her heart than any man had ever been.

He turned away and headed out the door. "Welcome to Greece."

GIANNIS'S DRIVER COLLECTED Maggie and Nick in front of their apartment building. As they drove through the city, Nick felt strangely conflicted. The sights, smells, sounds were all so familiar on one level and so painful on another. No doubt, the prospect of seeing Stephano Kythos at Giannis's party had him on edge.

Nick reached into his jacket pocket and felt for the Heart of Artemis necklace. He wasn't sure why he'd brought it along tonight other than it somehow helped him feel closer to Yanni, Kyrena and the kids.

"It's different at night," Maggie said, looking out the window. Daytime outdoor cafés had become fashionable clubs with people overflowing onto the streets.

Nick let the necklace drop to the bottom of his pocket and focused for a moment on Maggie. He'd been surprised to see her looking so feminine tonight, in high-heeled sandals and a sundress with a lacy wrap around her shoulders. What kind of man would care about a city when he had such a lovely woman sitting next to him? What kind of man would wish she wasn't here? Was he an idiot for his single-minded approach toward honor and revenge?

No. She was simply hell on his concentration. There'd be time enough for indulgences after he avenged Yanni's murder. Simple as that.

They drove through Sýndagma, where the main government buildings were located, then started uphill on a narrow road to the foot of Mount Lykavitós. The higher they drove, the more expansive the view. In a few hours it would be dark and all they'd be able to see would be a mass of blinking lights. Since the sun hadn't set, the houses situated on the slopes could still view the Acropolis and National Gardens.

Near the top, Maggie glanced behind them. "Is that all pollution?"

Nick turned to see the typical haze hanging over the city and nodded. "It's worst in July and August. Especially if there's no wind. But look." He pointed westward. "You can kind of see the mountains of the Peloponnese in the distance."

"How far is that?"

"One hundred and fifty, maybe two hundred kilometers as the crow flies."

"Giannis lives on this hillside?"

Nick nodded. "This area is called Kolonáki. If you have money to burn, there's no place better to do it."

They turned off the main, twisting road, drove through a wrought-iron gate and onto a circular drive. The Ramos residence was made of light stone with a tiled roof and a large, well-lit pool off to the side. Several luxury automobiles lined the drive, but their car stopped at the wide front steps.

Nick's stomach turned. The last time he'd been face to face with Stephano Kythos had been in an Athens courtroom when Nick had testified on Kyrena's behalf. Stephano had been manipulative and vindictive. How Nick would love to see Stephano's reaction to seeing Yanni and Kyrena's Heart of Artemis.

Spontaneously pulling the necklace out of his pocket, he turned to Maggie. "Do me a favor?" As soon as the words left his mouth, he realized he shouldn't be involving Maggie in the mess. "Never mind." He moved to put the necklace back into his pocket.

"Wait a minute!" Maggie reached for the rich gold pendant glittering in the fading light and held it against her palm. "It's beautiful." She studied the delicate filigree box with its small heart suspended inside. "You were going to ask me to wear it, weren't you?"

"Yes, but it's not important." Before he could put the necklace back into his pocket, Maggie snatched it out of his hand.

She drew the chain over her head, hopped out of the car, and took off for the house. "Come on, let's go."

He shot after her. "Maggie, don't—" The front door opened and a servant greeted Maggie. Nick jogged to catch up with her and whispered in her ear, "Take that necklace off."

"You wanted me to wear it, so I am."

Giannis came into the foyer. So much for getting the pendant back. "Nick, you're late." There was no accusation in Giannis's tone, only concern in the frown lining his jowly cheeks.

"My apologies." Nick bowed his head. "It was a long flight."

"Uneventful, I hope," Giannis said. "Marie's been practically pacing the floors waiting for you." He turned to Maggie and shook her hand. "Miss Dillon. Welcome to Greece."

"Thank you, Minister."

"Please, Giannis in my home."

"Giannis. Call me Maggie."

"If Marie finds you two have arrived and I've not brought you to her, she'll never forgive me. Come." He motioned for them to follow. Nick glanced around, remembering nearly every nook and cranny in their house. He'd played here as a child when his parents had come for dinner parties.

They were led down a corridor, past a large room filled with people, and on to a smaller room at the back of the house. "She prefers a quiet, intimate setting and tends to barricade herself in our patio," Giannis explained.

"I can see why," Maggie said. "It's beautiful out here."

The area was still and quiet, despite the rumblings in the rest of the house. Richly hand-painted ceramic tiles in a leafy green pattern covered the floor, and evening sunlight filtered through the vine-wrapped arbor, casting those underneath in warm, yellow highlights.

"Is that Santorini?" Maggie asked, pointing toward a fresco of a curved, volcanic island beach scene.

"Very good," Giannis said. "It is the most popular of our islands."

Nick noticed Marie standing on the other side of the patio surrounded by a small group of people. She'd barely changed. Instead of making her seem old, the silver streaks through her thick black hair only made her appear more elegant.

She glanced up. "Nicholas!" She ran to him, wrapped her arms around his shoulders, and, standing on the tips of her toes, lavished several kisses on each of his cheeks. Abruptly she stepped back. Her smile was wide and bright, her eyes tender. "Look at you. You've grown old since I last saw you."

"Hopefully not too old, Marie." He chuckled. "You look as chipper as a Persian squirrel."

"Ah, that smirk. Those mischievous eyes. Just as I remember. All the young tourist girls flirted shamelessly with you. One look and they were yours. Is that how you convinced this innocent young woman into business with you?"

"Innocent?" Nick laughed. "She talked me into working with her. This is Maggie Dillon, Marie."

"Smart. And beautiful." With raised eyebrows, Marie glanced at Nick before returning to Maggie. She clasped her warm fingers around Maggie's outstretched hand.

"Nice to meet you, Marie," Maggie said.

"As a friend of Nick's you're welcome in my home at any time. Now, Nick. Tell me what you have been doing all these years."

Marie and Giannis questioned him intently about the intricacies of his shipping business and the plans for his new business venture. Nick, in turn, asked several questions about their children and how Giannis's recent government appointment had affected their lives. Maggie stood politely next to him, appearing to enjoy listening to all the information passing back and forth.

"And Kyrena? How is she?" Marie whispered.

"Marie!" Giannis cautioned in hushed tones. "I asked you not to discuss her."

"And why not? Kyrena played with my daughters day in and day out. I have a right to know how she's doing." Marie looked offended. "Besides, Stephano is married now. He must be over that nonsense." She turned back to Nick. "So Kyrena. How is she?"

"She's very happy, Marie," Nick offered quietly.

"And Nestor and Christine?"

"Growing fast. You'd be proud of them. They do well in school and make friends easily. I'll send pictures when I get home."

"Okay, that's enough," Giannis said. "Marie, why don't you introduce Maggie to some of our other guests?"

Marie hooked her arm through Maggie's. "First we must get you some of my wonderfully rich coffee..."

Nick smiled as Maggie looked back at him. It was clear as those beautiful eyes on her face that she wanted to hear what Giannis had to say. Strangely enough, after all the time they'd spent together in her office, he'd become accustomed to having her nearby. Her absence felt like a chill in the air.

"Have you seen Stephano?" Giannis's serious tone pulled Nick back.

"No." He was curious what Stephano's reaction

would be to seeing the Heart of Artemis, but courtesy toward Giannis won out. "Now that I've seen Marie, maybe I should leave before I run into him."

"That's not necessary. I told him you were coming, and he's assured me he won't pursue charges against you. Or Kyrena. He said it's time to heal, not hate."

Easier said than done.

"I called your father after we met in Washington," Giannis went on. "He thinks you're still looking for Yanni's killer, and, I have to admit, so do I."

Nick glanced off into the garden and slowly exhaled. "What do you want me to say?"

"It's why you're here, isn't it?"

"Yes."

"Then I ask you to step back and let us do our job."

"You've had five years. How much longer is it going to take?"

"One minute of patience, ten years of peace." Giannis relayed an old Greek saying. "It will not be long, Nick. Not long."

Unfortunately, Nick's patience had run out the day he'd signed Kyrena's divorce papers.

"This situation is sensitive, complicated," Giannis went on. "You may be getting yourself into something for which you're not prepared."

"Such as?"

"The man who placed the bomb in Yanni's car isn't a terrorist."

"I know that. He's a hired assassin."

"And a highly trained one, at that. What if you're killed looking for him?"

Nick stubbornly rested his arms across his chest. "So be it."

Giannis narrowed his eyes. "This man is believed responsible for the deaths of scores of people. Many of whom were innocent bystanders. The wives and children of his targets. He kills without conscience."

"What's your point?"

"Have you given no thought to what you've gotten Miss Dillon involved in?"

"Maggie has nothing to do with this. She's my business partner. Nothing more, nothing less."

"Does she know why you're here? What if she inadvertently gets involved? What if Gavras tries to use her to get to you?"

"She won't be involved," Nick said, emphasizing each word. "Maggie has nothing to do with my personal affairs, and I would appreciate you passing that on to any interested parties."

"There are many people involved, Nick, who've spent years accumulating evidence on this case. It would help tremendously if you could positively identify the assassin. And then step away." Giannis closed his eyes for a moment and sighed, appearing weary of the discussion. "Can you identify him?"

"I can't, Giannis," he lied. "It was long ago, and I didn't see the man very clearly."

Berk Tarik belonged to Nick.

CHAPTER ELEVEN

"Is THERE SOMETHING WRONG with the coffee?" Maggie would have been uncomfortable with Marie's intense scrutiny if the older woman's gaze hadn't been so non-threatening. There was a definite degree of motherly protectiveness in those knowing eyes.

"Oh, no, it's wonderful," Maggie said. "The meal was delicious, and now I'm just…rather full."

In truth, Marie's Greek coffee was awful—grainy, bitter, and strong enough to put hair on anyone's chest. Maggie had managed to sip away at the first cup, distracted as she was with meeting Marie's daughters, their husbands and several guests at the dinner party. This second serving, though, was bound to be the death of her.

"Then don't finish it."

"You wouldn't be offended?"

"Offended?" Marie's elegant features appeared out of place scrunched up in a quizzical expression. Then awareness seemed to dawn. "You don't enjoy Greek coffee."

With an apologetic smile, Maggie shook her head.

"Why, then, have you had two cups?"

"I thought it was impolite not to drink at least three."

"Did Nick put you up to that?" Marie's shoulders shook with laughter. "He was always pulling tricks as a child."

"That doesn't sound like Nick."

"No," Marie said. "I suppose life—and death—has a way of sobering us up."

Wasn't that the truth. "I'm fairly certain I read it in a guidebook."

"Well, if you're offered coffee again, Maggie, simply ask for something else." Marie grasped Maggie's wrist. "Will you be all right?"

"I'll be fine." Maggie managed a chuckle herself.

A brief silence hung between them. Maggie had been waiting for the opportunity to ask a few questions about Kyrena, but there wasn't going to be a perfect opening. She was going to have to jump in before Nick and Giannis rejoined them.

"So you've been friends with Nick's family for years."

Marie nodded slowly, as if reminiscing. "We spent much of our time at a lovely oceanfront home in Glyfada near the Ballos family. There are some nights, here in Athens, I would give almost anything for those cool seaside breezes."

"And Kyrena? She was a neighbor, as well?" Maggie asked, hoping to sound casual.

Marie lowered her voice as her gaze scanned the crowd. "Kyrena was the daughter of a Kythos housekeeper. There was quite a bit of talk when they announced their engagement. She's the reason Yanni's father disinherited him."

"Because she was a housekeeper's daughter?"

"He thought she was after the Kythos fortune and was sure she wouldn't go through with the wedding as soon as he wrote Yanni out of his will."

"But it didn't make a difference."

"Of course not. They were in love." One of Marie's

daughters came and whispered in Marie's ear. "I'm sorry, Maggie. Apparently, we have a minor crisis I must attend to in the kitchen."

"Go. I'll be fine."

Relieved at the prospect of not having to say or do anything, Maggie relaxed and glanced around. There had to be more than fifty people at the party. From across the room, a woman caught Maggie's gaze and approached. "You must be Maggie Dillon. I've heard so much about you."

The young woman, with thick black hair falling straight to her shoulders and alert brown eyes, was nothing short of stunning. She had to be a model or an actress. "And you are?"

"Talia Kythos. My husband is an old friend of Nick's."

"Stephano's wife." Maggie forced a smile. "Nice to meet you."

"You're working for Giannis in the government buildings at Sýndagma?"

"Yes." Maggie nodded.

"Then we should meet for lunch, or coffee. I often accompany my husband volunteering at the Ministry of Culture, organizing events. Shall I call on you if I'm in the area?" The offer seemed almost desperate.

"That'd be nice," Maggie heard herself saying.

Talia noticed Nick's pendant and her smile dimmed. "Where did you get that?"

"From Nick. Why?"

"I was under the impression there were only two of these in the world." Talia moved closer and reached toward her. "May I?"

"Sure." Maggie drew the chain away from her chest, causing the pendant to swing from her hand.

Talia cupped the small box in her palm and studied it. "It seems genuine. The Heart of Artemis."

"Excuse me?"

"Some believe this pendant to be thousands of years old." Talia glanced down at Maggie. "Are you familiar with its history?"

"No."

"Stephano's mother said this pendant holds the key to life." Talia took one last look at the necklace, then let it go. "She told me a myth I'd never heard."

This, Maggie had to hear. "I love Greek myths."

"Then you've heard of Artemis, daughter of Zeus and maiden goddess of the hunt?"

Maggie nodded.

"Well, then you probably know the generally accepted stories about Artemis. How she vowed to remain chaste, pure, a virgin."

"Let me guess," Maggie said with a chuckle. "She didn't."

"Not if we're to believe a little-known story." Talia hid her grin as she took a sip of red wine. "One that didn't survive in most writings."

"Okay," Maggie said. "I'll bite. What happened?"

"It all began with Artemis hearing tales of a great hunter, a Cretan named Siproites. For years, Artemis watched him from afar, protected him, admired him. Siproites, for his part, pledged to worship only Artemis, claiming her beauty and prowess was matched by no other goddess.

"Of course, this angered Aphrodite, who'd always been jealous of Artemis, her half sister. Over and over, Aphrodite tried to trick Siproites into falling in love with her, but he stayed true to Artemis."

"That must have pissed off Aphrodite even more."

"She grew to hate Siproites." Talia frowned as if the tale saddened her. "As the days passed, Artemis came to Crete more and more often to be near Siproites. One day, she was bathing near his hunting grounds, grew tired and fell asleep naked at the water's edge."

"Aphrodite found her."

"You're good at this." Talia smiled. "Seeing an opportunity, she placed a spell on Siproites and led him to where Artemis lay sleeping. Under Aphrodite's spell, he didn't recognize the sleeping beauty and made love to her."

"Uh, oh."

"Exactly. Artemis had been known to kill men for lesser offenses." Talia's brow creased. "When Artemis awoke and realized what had happened she was furious. But she…"

"Couldn't kill Siproites," Maggie said.

"No. She couldn't harm her one and only love."

"And Aphrodite was watching," Maggie guessed.

"And waiting." Talia nodded. "Artemis was now pregnant. As she grew with child, she was frightened Zeus would notice, so she isolated herself on the island of Delos. After giving birth to a boy, she brought him to Siproites and left them, promising to love them forever.

"Aphrodite told Zeus and he went off in a rage that any mortal man would take his daughter's virginity. Artemis fought with her father. Zeus finally agreed, for his daughter's sake, not to kill her lover and son. Instead, he caged Siproites and the child and banished them to the heavens."

Maggie touched the box pendant with its dangling heart.

"Artemis would often sneak away to visit them, but

she could never open the cage. One day, knowing she would never love again, Artemis cut out her useless heart," Talia said, glimmers of unshed tears in her eyes, "and threw it into the sky where Siproites is said to have caught it in his golden cage." Talia looked at the pendant. "The door opened and Siproites and her son were freed."

"The key to life is love," Maggie said, mesmerized. "And without a heart, Artemis could never love again."

Talia took a deep breath, as if coming out of a trance. "I hate those tragic stories, but they're a lot like train wrecks, you know? You can't help but be fascinated."

"Exactly."

"Those necklaces have been in my husband's family for centuries, and my mother-in-law gave one to each of her sons. I was under the impression that Yanni gave his to Kyrena. She must've given it to Nick."

"And Stephano?"

"He told me his had been lost." She looked away. "But I've seen it hidden in his private safe."

Though she'd only just met Talia, Maggie couldn't help but feeling pity for this beautiful woman, so obviously living her own Greek tragedy. Stephano must be one horse's ass.

"There you are." A man, like a Greek god, facial features and stature all perfectly proportioned, came to stand next to Talia, putting his hand possessively at the small of her back.

Talia smiled up at him. "This is Maggie, Stephano. Nick Ballos's business partner."

Finally, she'd get to meet Yanni's brother.

"Pleasure to meet you, Maggie." Stephano may

have politely extended his hand, but as Talia continued talking, Maggie felt Stephano's gaze absorbing her, taking in every strand of her hair, every seam in her clothing, missing nothing. He made her feel exposed and vulnerable. She glanced up at him just as he settled, for an imperceptible moment, on the Heart of Artemis.

Then she felt a warm hand on her arm, looked up into Nick's face and immediately relaxed. "You okay?" he asked.

She nodded.

When Nick turned to Stephano it was if a match had been flicked onto fuel-soaked coals. Maggie didn't care what Nick had said about his neutral feelings for Yanni's brother. These two men were enemies. It was as obvious in the cool lack of emotion on Stephano's face as in the hostility surfacing on Nick's rough features. The underlying current of emotions finally caught up with Maggie. She was exhausted.

"Stephano," Nick said, nodding his head.

"Hello, Nick. My wife, Talia."

"Pleased to meet you." Nick was clearly doing his best to be cordial, but Stephano's presence was throwing him.

"I guess I'm more tired than I thought," Maggie said, giving him an out. "Are you ready to go, Nick?"

He glanced down at her and his eyes softened. "Sure."

"Pleasure meeting you, Talia. Stephano."

Talia raised her glass and smiled.

They'd only gone a few steps when Nick turned back toward Stephano and said, "I *will* find Yanni's killer."

And then what, Maggie wondered.

"That sounds like a threat," Stephano said.

"Take it any way you want."

DESPITE MAGGIE ATTEMPTING to rally and make conversation, Nick barely said a word the entire drive back to their apartments. Whatever his reasons for coming to Greece, they were pulling him down into a place so dark she was afraid she soon wouldn't be able to reach him.

"Are you okay?" she asked him once they'd left Giannis's driver and stepped onto the sidewalk.

"I'm fine. A lot on my mind."

When they reached their respective apartment doors, Maggie remembered the necklace. "Here." She took it off and held it out to him. "Stephano noticed it, but he didn't show much of a reaction."

He pocketed the gold chain.

"Talia, though, seemed…saddened that I was wearing it."

"Why?"

"She told me the myth."

"Siproites and Artemis."

"And she said Stephano keeps his pendant locked in his personal safe."

"He should've given it to his wife. That was the intent. I'm guessing he's still not over Kyrena."

"The key to life…"

"Is love. Any fool knows that." He reached out and brushed his fingertips across her cheek. "Good night, Maggie."

So who was the fool? *Stay with me*, she wanted to say. *Hold me. Make love to me. I feel lonely and alone in this strange country. Like you. Let's finish what we started the other night.*

His hesitation told her he was thinking the same thing, only Kate was here. Maggie might be a bad example in a lot of ways, but she'd always been careful around Kate with regard to her relationships with men. She wasn't about to slip up now, not with everything Kate was going through.

"Night, Nick." She'd no sooner stepped into her flat and thrown her purse onto the countertop than a brisk knock sounded on the apartment door. Maggie peered through the peephole and opened the door. Nick stood with his suitcase in his hand, clothes hanging out the edges. He'd thrown his things into the bag and folded it without bothering to tuck in the edges.

"I can't stay over there," he said. "I'm coming in."

"What's going on?" She stepped back.

"Those guys?" He came through the door. "The A-Team you so affectionately call them? They're slobs."

"You can't stay here."

"Why not?"

"Because it's only a two-bedroom, and Kate's a blue-ribbon bed hog. How bad is it next door?"

"Have *you* ever lived with the A-Team?" He worked the knot on his tie. "Go check it out."

Maggie marched over to the A-Team's flat and pounded on the door. Alex answered. "Maggie McGee. Wassup?"

"What did you guys do to make Nick leave?"

"Nick's gone?" he said, surprised. "Since when?"

"Since he came over to my apartment a second ago."

"We did nothing. Trust me. *Nada.*"

"Yeah, right." She brushed past Alex and stepped into the kitchen area. Takeout containers littered the countertops. Whatever had been left in the coffeepot was charred to a crisp and emitting an awful odor. Dirty dishes, encrusted with God knows what, were piled high in the sink. And someone, she didn't want to know who, was making rude noises in the bathroom down the hall. "You guys are disgusting."

"That's genius for ya."

"Well, Einstein, if I lose the damage deposit on this crib, I'm taking it out of your fees."

"Whatever."

She headed back to the other flat and found Nick in his boxers with his shirt hanging open. Damn, he looked good. "You're right," she said. "They're pigs."

"I'll sleep on your couch for tonight and look into a hotel tomorrow." He headed to the living room.

"You won't fit." There had to be close to a foot discrepancy between his height and what was suddenly looking an awful lot like a love seat. "Come on, you can sleep in my room." She led the way down the hall. "I'll bunk with Kate." After grabbing what she needed out of her suitcase, she turned.

Nick stood between her and the door, looking thoroughly exhausted. What would happen if she smoothed his forehead, rubbed the tension out of his shoulders? The image of being pulled into some kind of vortex along with him flashed through her mind. Good thing Kate was here, or Maggie may have jumped right along with him into the big black hole.

"Good night, Nick." She snuck by him, closing her eyes against the up-close shot at his bare chest and abs.

"Night, Maggie."

She crossed the hall and went into Kate's room. Her sister was spread-eagle on the bed, snuffling like a baby. Maggie glanced behind her. Nick was already lying down, apparently out cold the moment his head had hit the pillow.

"Perfect. Just perfect."

CHAPTER TWELVE

THEIR MEETINGS Monday morning at the Ministry of Public Order went as smooth as clockwork. After being introduced to the relevant staff in the departments involved in the project, Maggie, Nick and the A-Team set up shop in a conference room and got to work. Maggie analyzed the project requirements, and the group got hot and heavy into programming.

True to his word, Nick gave the project his complete attention from day one, although he had a hard time finding a hotel nearby with a vacancy.

"Stay with us," Maggie had said. "I slept fine with Kate."

He agreed, and after a few days, it seemed as if the arrangement had worked out for the best. Nick had a way of drawing Kate out, if only a little, and he was clearly content with their company. As far as Maggie was concerned, though, having Nick around twenty-four-seven was a mixed bag. She was having a hard time keeping an appropriate level of detachment.

On one hand, she appreciated the sight of him coming out of the bathroom with a towel wrapped around his waist, tying his tie in the kitchen, or sitting at the counter reading the Athens daily paper while waiting for her to get ready in the morning. On the other hand, it was becoming increasingly more difficult to keep her distance. Her only distraction was work.

Overall, it was a good thing Maggie had insisted on coming to Greece, and it was going to be another week before she could leave the A-Team alone and head back to D.C. for a few days. Her only dilemma was figuring out what to do with Kate.

By late afternoon Friday, Maggie, as well as everyone else, had already clocked more than sixty hours on the job and was ready to throw in the towel a bit early to let off some steam. When they all piled out of the cab back at their apartment building, Maggie said to no one in particular, "So what's everyone doing tonight?"

Alex immediately piped up. "We're hitting Exhária. The club scene is supposed to be hot. Wanna come along?"

Clubs. "No thanks." She glanced at Nick. "I'm going to see if I can talk Kate into doing something with me. Want to get out with us? See a few things?"

"Sorry to be a drag, Maggie, but I've already got plans tonight. You and Kate enjoy yourself."

When they got back to the apartment, Kate was on the couch watching MTV. It was one of the few English channels they could get at the apartment. "Hey, Kate."

No response. Nick shrugged at Maggie and went down the hall to his room.

This silent treatment was older than old. "Want to get some fresh air tonight? Check out the Acropolis, or the Agora, get a nice meal?"

"No."

"Kate, we're going be here for at least a few more

days. You might as well take advantage of those group tour packages I bought for you. Did you go to any of them this week?"

Again, no response.

"You can't sit here and veg the whole time."

"Wanna bet?"

"You're in Greece. Check it out." Maggie opened the drapes to their spectacular view of the Parthenon.

"I don't want to be in Greece," Kate said. "I want to be back in D.C. making pots for Rufus's exhibition."

"I thought some time away would help you to see things more clearly."

"You can't keep me here forever." Kate stood. "I already told Rufus I'm taking the internship, whether you agree to it or not. So if I'm not back home in time to start when he needs me, I promise, I will hate you for the rest of my life."

Now there was a big fat line being drawn, and what was Maggie's favorite thing to do with lines? "Well, I guess I'd better put on a damned thick skin then, 'cause that's an awful lot of hate."

Kate stalked out of the flat and slammed the door.

Well, Maggie thought ruefully, if nothing else, she'd gotten her sister out of the apartment. She had a momentary rush of concern over Kate on her own in Athens, but at least she wasn't back in D.C. partying. Besides, Maggie had no doubt Kate could take care of herself, despite not speaking the language. Maggie took a deep breath and stepped onto the balcony, feeling definitely at a loose end. She was in Athens with nothing to do and no one to do it with.

Nick's voice sounded through the sliding door to his bedroom. His words were somewhat muted, but she could tell he was on his phone. "I've got some time now," he said, pausing. "I'll be there in half an hour."

He had his own agenda all right, and there was no better time for Maggie to find out exactly what it was.

I HATE HER. I HATE HER. I HATE HER.

Kate strode out of the apartment building and double-timed it down the street, her gaze focused on the cobblestone at her feet, her thoughts scattered. Yes, Kate had gone on the tours Maggie had organized for her. And, yes, much to her own chagrin, she'd enjoyed every one of them, especially the National Archaeological Museum. But, no, she was absolutely not going to tell Maggie. Maggie was ruining Kate's life and Kate wasn't going to let her forget it.

"Stasee! Stasee. Stop!"

Kate looked up in barely enough time to keep herself from colliding with a man. She backed away. "Sorry."

"American?" he said, his accent rich and rolling.

She nodded.

"Always in such a hurry," he said. "You're in Greece now. Slow down. Savor. Enjoy."

"If you say so." She kept walking.

"What?" He walked alongside her. "You're not liking your visit to my country?"

"No."

"Impossible. Where you have been?"

"Lots of places, and they all bite. I don't want to be here."

"Don't want to be here? In this wonderful city? You're not here on vacation? With your family?"

"No. My sister's here for work. And dragged me along."

"You're staying with her, here at these apartments?"

"Yeah. With her and her stupid…boyfriend or whatever he is."

"Then come with me to the Agora. We'll shop, eat, drink some *ouzo*. Enjoy!" He stopped and spread his arms wide. "Let me help you make lemons out of your lemonade."

She laughed. "You mean lemonade out of lemons?"

His expression turned quizzical. He was too old for her, but he was hot, one of the nicest people Kate had met since coming to this loser country. What could it hurt to have some fun? Maggie sure as hell didn't need to know.

NICK LEFT THE BUILDING and grabbed a cab. "Omónia Square." He gave the driver the address and glanced at the road behind him to make sure he wasn't being followed. Seeing no one suspicious, he turned back around and watched the city scenes zipping by his window.

Northwest out of Sýndagma, grand avenues and mainstream retailers gave way to outdoor markets, bazaars and smaller shops. The Omónia area may have been forced to clean up its act, but the city's old red-light district had, nonetheless, retained its gritty, working-class atmosphere.

Not long after he'd left the apartment, Nick arrived at his destination. He paid his driver and entered a jewelry shop on the corner, passing two security guards positioned near the door, both of them big, hulking men. He nodded at them and proceeded to the back of the store.

"Angelo!" Nick found his father's friend sitting behind the display cases.

The old, balding man turned and smiled. "Nick, it's so good to see you again." He opened a section of the counter. "Come back here." They embraced and Nick bent to kiss his wrinkly cheeks. "*Kathome*. Sit."

"How have you been?" Nick sat down in the chair opposite Angelo, feeling antsy. In fulfilling his promise to Maggie that her business would come first, he'd had to wait several days for this. Now that he was here, he wanted information, yesterday.

"I'm well. Getting old, though." Angelo sighed and glanced out the window, forever watchful. "Almost ready to retire like your father." He pulled a file from a nearby cabinet. "This is all I have. Not much more than when we last talked."

"Thank you."

"There is someone else you could try. He may give you some information."

Nick glanced up.

"A police officer who worked Yanni's case for some time. He's semiretired now. Works in Thíva as a security guard."

"North of Athens?"

"Yes. He was reluctant to give me anything, but this is personal for you. If you go to see him, he may be persuaded."

"His name?"

"Cosmo Papadakis. I'll tell him you're coming."

"I'll head there this weekend."

"The sooner the better."

"Why?"

Angelo sighed. "My man who's been in Syria watching Tarik, says that Tarik flew to Athens only a day after you arrived."

"Coincidence?"

"He doesn't leave Syria for months, then he happens

to come to Athens the day after you do?" Angelo slowly shook his head. "That's no coincidence. Besides, he's been watching you here and there, outside your apartment building, at the government buildings. Not all the time. Enough for us to notice."

It had already started. Nick rubbed his tired eyes. "Why is *he* following *me*?"

"Perhaps he got wind of you looking for him."

"So why wouldn't he stay in familiar territory, set a trap, and wait for me to walk into it?"

"It's best to observe your enemies, for they first find your faults."

"Has your man noticed any of Stephano's people following me?"

"No." That surprised Nick. "Someone did follow you here, though." Angelo flicked his head toward the street.

He felt backed into a corner. If Tarik didn't get him, Stephano probably would. No matter what Stephano wanted the world to believe, the man had never forgiven Nick for taking Kyrena and the children out of Greece. "I thought I was free and clear." Nick stifled the impulse to turn and look outside. "Did you see him?"

"No." Angelo shook his head. "The same taxi drove by twice. He's now parked across the street." Angelo nodded toward the guards at the front of the store. "I can have Stamos and my American friend, Riley, do something about him."

"No. I can take care of it. Do you have that package for me?"

Angelo glanced out the window again and stood. "Come. In back."

Nick followed him inside a storage room.

Angelo placed a stepstool at one end of the shelving

units, reached for the top shelf, and brought down a black case. He opened it to reveal an array of weapons. "Will this be sufficient?"

"I'm not going after an army."

"Are you sure?"

MAGGIE PAID HER DRIVER, stepped onto the sidewalk, and slipped on a dark pair of sunglasses to shield her eyes from the hot, unrelenting sun. Nick had left the jewelry shop on foot and was already far ahead of her down the street. He rounded a corner over a block away.

Now where was he going?

Her taxi zoomed back into the flow of traffic and Maggie had no choice. One way or another, she was going to find out what he was doing. Amid the mass of pedestrians and milling shoppers, she ran to catch up with Nick. She turned into the alleyway. It was virtually deserted. She saw Nick's back an instant before he turned again. Running after him, she stopped at the corner and peeked around the stuccoed wall. It was a narrow passageway. Deserted. And Nick was nowhere in sight.

In for a penny, in for a pound.

She took a few steps. It felt like a hallway between buildings and it seemed to almost close in on her. She gained speed on nearing the end of the passageway. Someone gripped her upper arm, yanked her back into a dark doorway, and slammed her face first against the wall.

She opened her mouth to scream, but the wind had been knocked out of her. She struggled against the hands banding her wrists against the wall. It was useless. She couldn't move.

"Maggie? What the hell?"

At the sound of Nick's voice, her fear instantly turned

to rage. He flipped her around, and she slammed her heel into his foot. His hand left her mouth, his arm loosened.

"What was that for?" Nick bent over and held his injured foot.

"For scaring me half to death."

"You were following me, remember?"

"What are you doing?"

"Maybe this was all about getting you alone." He grabbed her hand again and pressed her against the wall. He bent his head as if to kiss her.

"So now we're on again," she breathed.

"I have no idea." His mouth was so close, too close. "You confuse the hell out of me."

"That makes two of us."

His mouth was on her, kissing her. She should pull away, but the wall was cold and hard against her back, and Nick felt so warm. He deepened their contact, slanting his head and running his tongue along hers. She groaned. At least she thought the sound had come from her. Maybe it had been him.

Who cared? His grip on her hands loosened and she wrapped her arms around his neck. He pulled back, set her away from him, and glanced down the passageway. "This is a very bad idea. On so many levels."

She felt dazed, cold. "What?" She blinked, recovering.

"Come on. We need to go." He headed toward the street. "There might be someone following me."

"That was me."

"You sure there was no one else?"

"No, I'm not sure. Why would someone else be following you? What were you doing in that jewelry shop?" She went after him. "What's going on, Nick?"

"This doesn't have anything to do with you, Maggie."

"It does if it's going to affect my company's project."

"Your project won't be impacted. I give you my word."

"Do you ever let anyone in?"

"No."

"Nick, stop!" He was driving her crazy. She grabbed his arm before he could leave the passageway. "Can I help?"

He looked down at her then, surprise registering on his face. "No," he said, more softly. "No one can help."

"Is this about your friend, Yanni?"

He glanced at her hand on his arm, then something seemed to give. "Yes," he said, turning away for a second.

"You said he was killed in a car accident. That's only part of it, isn't it?"

"Look, I'll do your work for you. I'll get your job done. What I do in my free time is my own business."

"That's not fair. Whether you want me there or not, I'm in your life." She couldn't believe she was saying this. In such a short amount of time, she'd connected with Nick in a way she hadn't with any other man.

"No promises," he said. "No commitments, remember?"

"I want to know what you're planning."

"His death was suspicious, so I'm gathering information."

"Then what?"

He stood silent. He'd given her his word that what he was doing wouldn't affect her company's project, and she wanted with everything in her to believe him. "Then you'll turn this over to the police," she said. "Right?"

"Right."

She'd gotten the answer she was after, but, for some reason, it didn't come close to satisfying her.

CHAPTER THIRTEEN

NICK CAME DOWN THE HALL, yawning and scratching his head. Surprisingly, Kate was already awake and sitting on the couch. She didn't bother glancing up from her laptop when he went into the kitchen to make some coffee.

"Where's Maggie?" he asked. Funny, she was the last thing he thought of before falling asleep at night and the first thing that popped into his mind on waking.

"She said something totally stupid about checking out the Greek patisseries *on this fine Saturday morning*."

Holding back a smile, he scooped fresh grounds into a filter. "When's she going to be back?"

"How would I know, and why should I care?"

The response was dead-on Kate. She had to be the most sullen, bad-tempered, and moody teenager he'd ever met. She was also incredibly talented and creative and stubborn enough to make something of it. And he liked her.

"What'd you do last night?" he asked. She had to be getting bored out of her mind. There was only so much MTV anyone with half a brain could stand.

"Went to the agora, hung out. Why?"

"Wondering how you're keeping yourself busy. Staying safe, right?" Teenagers had no clue how vulnerable they were in their own cities, let alone a foreign country. "There are a lot of creeps out there who prey on tourists."

"I can take care of myself, thank you very much."

"I'm sure you can." He filled the coffeemaker with water. "Even so, I checked something out for you." Before she could veil her true feelings, he witnessed the complete despair in her eyes. "Promise not to tell Maggie?" he asked.

"We're not talking. How could I tell her anything?"

He opened his briefcase on the counter, pulled out a business card and laid it on the coffee table in front of Kate. "There's a potter's studio down the road."

She didn't have to speak. The excitement in her eyes said it all.

"I talked with the owner."

She put her laptop aside and sat forward. "Will they let me rent some space?"

"He's behind on his orders and could use some help. Go show him what you can do, and he might hire you."

Kate ran over and hugged him. "I'm sorry for all the bad things I ever said about you."

He laughed. Yep, he really liked this kid.

THE GREEKS WEREN'T big on breakfast, and since Maggie could barely function on an empty stomach one of her first discoveries had been a *zaharoplastío*, a cross between a café and a bakery, a block from the flat. Carrying a bag of *loukoumádhes*, deep-fried pastries sprinkled with cinnamon she and Kate had developed a taste for, and *baklavá*, honey-soaked layers of dough all the guys seemed to enjoy, and fresh, locally made yogurt for Nick, she had something for the whole crew.

When she got back to the apartment, Kate was gone and Nick was coming out of his bedroom, dressed in cargo shorts and a white T-shirt, his hair damp and disheveled.

"Morning." She set her bags on the countertop and grabbed the yogurt container. "I got this for you."

"Thank you." Nick poured some coffee into a travel mug. "And good morning to you, too."

"Going somewhere?" she asked.

"Road trip. I'll be back this afternoon."

"Oh." She hadn't meant to sound disappointed. It just came out that way.

"Do you have plans?" he asked.

"Not yet." Since it was Saturday morning, and the government offices were closed, there wasn't a lot she could accomplish work-wise. Shannon was doing quite well holding down the fort in D.C., and with Kate still being Kate, and the A-Team sleeping off massive hangovers—she'd checked before heading out for treats—Maggie had no clue what she might do. "I'll think of something," she said brightly.

"I could hire you a tour guide," he offered. "Or you could head out on your own. The three most popular destinations in these parts are the Parthenon, the Acropolis and the Agora. That'd keep you busy an entire weekend."

"Don't worry about me. I'll be fine." Although a *road trip*, with the implied possibilities of seeing some of the natural countryside, did sound much more interesting than the Acropolis. "Did you know there are supposed to be 190 species of orchids in Greece?" Somehow, that slipped out.

Nick looked down at her and frowned. "I'll make a deal with you. I have some business in Thíva that won't take me long. Come with me, and then afterward, I'll take you sightseeing. I'll be your personal tour guide for the afternoon."

"That's okay. You don't need to take care of me. Anyway, I should stick around in case Kate comes back."

"I'm not taking care of you, Maggie," he said. "And Kate's gone for the rest of the day."

"How do you know? Where is she?"

He hesitated. "I checked out a potter and his studio down the street. She's helping him out."

Maggie was actually relieved that Kate would be keeping herself busy. "Thank you."

"I figured you'd be mad."

"You did it anyway?"

He laughed. "Take a break. I want you to come with me today."

"Really?"

"Really."

"Well, when you put it that way." She grabbed her bag. "Let's go."

"WE'RE HERE." After having made sure they hadn't been followed out of Athens, Nick parked the rented Mercedes on the street at the address Angelo had given him for Cosmo Papadakis. The home was modest and unremarkable, and could've been situated in Phoenix, for all the personality of this particular neighborhood.

Maggie glanced around. "Where's here?"

"Thíva." It was a modern town. There was neither a ruin, nor museum in sight.

"I hope this isn't where you'd planned on sightseeing," she said, sounding completely disgusted.

"Hey, this city was built over ancient Thebes." He grinned. "And we're not far from the route Oedipus trekked from Athens to Delphi."

"Doesn't quite work for me."

He chuckled. "Relax. It's not what I envisioned, either. This stop is business."

"Then where are we going? I'm only familiar with the southern coast."

"It's a surprise."

"I hate surprises. Hand over a travel guide and I'll chart us a course."

"I don't have a travel book. Trust me." He climbed out of the car. "I'll be back in half an hour. Wait here."

"No way." Maggie opened her door. "It's too hot." It was only ten o'clock and already ninety degrees in the shade. "I need some air." She motioned down the block.

"This won't take long." He waited until she was far enough away that he didn't have to worry about her following him in, and then went to the front door to ring the bell. A graying, trim and fit man, probably in his late sixties opened the door. "Cosmo Papadakis?"

"May I help you?"

"I hope so." In Greek, Nick explained who he was and why he was there. "I'm hoping you may be able to shed some light on an old Athens car bombing."

"I know the one you're talking about. Your friend called." The man's face was tanned and leathery from years in the hot Greek sun. His seemingly bored expression barely changed as he considered Nick's request. "Come. I'll show you what I have." He led the way to a small room off the kitchen, an office. He sat down behind a tiny desk and opened a file cabinet drawer.

"Open cases," he explained. "The ones that stick in my mind. Every once in a while something comes to me. I make a call or two. Sometimes, it makes a difference." He pulled out a thin manila folder and shook his head. "The Yanni Kythos case is dead. At least to the Athens police. Not long after it happened, the Public Order people took all our files."

"Why?"

"Told us the jurisdiction had changed. A matter of national security."

"What do you think?"

"I think…they know who did it, and either they can't touch him, or they're building a case." He tossed his folder toward Nick. "You can look at what I kept, but you won't find much. I can tell you this for sure. Some pieces don't fit."

"Like?"

"It wasn't a terrorist, but someone put a lot of effort into making it look like it was, right down to the explosive trigger and materials. You probably already knew that."

Nick nodded.

"Another thing. Yanni's brother, Stephano, was at a conference in Paris when it happened."

"I flew to France myself and checked," Nick said. "Several eyewitnesses swore he was there."

"He was, yes. But he wasn't registered for the conference."

"What does that have to do with anything?"

"I'm not sure, but his flying out of town seemed sudden, as if he'd wanted an alibi."

"You think Stephano was behind the bombing?"

"That's another strange thing." Cosmo shook his head. "I was a detective with the Athens police for twenty years. You get to know when people are lying. Stephano Kythos seemed genuinely upset that his brother was dead."

"He never looked that heartbroken to me." Stephano was very powerful. Someone in the government could just as easily be trying to make a cast against him as covering it up. "Anything else?"

"Only what's in the file."

After thanking Cosmo, Nick stepped back outside to find Maggie leaning against the car. "Did you get what you came for?"

"No." All he had were more questions.

"How much longer?" Maggie asked, impatiently jiggling her foot.

"We'll be there shortly."

They'd driven a few hours out of Thíva through some of the most boring small industrial towns she'd ever seen. Good thing they were now heading into the foothills that had been in the distance for some time. They were driving along the craggy slopes of a steep mountain jutting out of the valley like a fist popping through the earth's crust and, suddenly, the landscape looked promising.

"Where are we?" she asked.

"Mount Parnassos."

The surrounding hillside was dotted with evergreens, towering cypress and low-lying junipers. Several ruins, set on a carpet of dry grasses and prickly-looking shrubs, were visible on the high mountain terraces.

"This all seems so rocky and barren," Maggie said, having expected the countryside to be full of wildflowers and lush vegetation. "Where the hell are all the orchids?"

He laughed. "It's summertime. Arid and hot in these parts. In the spring you'll see all kinds of colorful flowers. Cyclamen, poppies, orchids. And again in the autumn." He parked the rented car, grabbed a small pack and they climbed out. "Guess you'll have to come back another time of year."

She glanced around. "What is this place?"

"Delphi. This is what the ancient Greeks considered the belly button of the earth."

She followed him onto a path. "You're kidding, right?"

"Serious."

She should've known. Nick probably never kidded anyone.

"The ancient myths tell of Zeus releasing two eagles," he elaborated. "One to the east, one to the west. They collided at Delphi. But before that, Gaia, Mother Earth, was worshipped here. Then, according to myth, Apollo defeated her son, Python, at the sight of the temple. That battle marks the dawn of the Olympian gods."

"You mean Zeus, Hera, and the whole bunch?"

"Exactly."

They climbed some steps and zigzagged uphill through the ancient foundations of what had probably once been memorials. All the while, Nick pointed and explained, giving her, indeed, a tour. "It doesn't look like much now, but imagine that in its heyday there are believed to have been over three thousand gold, bronze and marble statues throughout these ruins."

"What happened to them all?"

"Greece's history is rife with conquerors. Mycenaeans and Venetians. Franks, Romans, Turks. They all walked off with pieces here and there."

When they got to the top, she turned around and the panoramic view took her breath away. The ruins looked out over a valley bordered by mountains on all except the farthest west side. "It feels as if we're at the top of the world," she said, pointing to a small, idyllic town near a huge bay of water. "What is that?"

"Itea. And that's the Gulf of Corinth. Pretty, isn't it?"

"Like a postcard. No wonder the ancient Greeks wanted to build here."

"This is where they constructed the Temple of Apollo." With a large theater on the hillside above them, Nick pointed at the rectangular ruins with several columns of varying heights rising at one end. "Know thyself," he said, turning thoughtful. "That's the saying that used to be encrypted over the temple's portal. About here." He waved over his head. "This was an important place. All kinds of people, commoners, heads of states, even kings, came to this exact spot to see Apollo's prophetess, the Oracle of Delphi. She would sit on a tripod in the temple, awaiting visitors. Her priestesses relayed questions and the oracle supposedly relayed Apollo's advice."

"Some kind of mystic or something?"

"Various high priestesses. For more than a thousand years, people came here from all over the world seeking counsel."

"That must have been some pretty accurate advice."

"This area was a political center of sorts, so priestesses were very knowledgeable about world events. I suppose if a person is vague enough, you can make it sound as if you're foretelling almost anything. A lot of the advice was very strange stuff. Then again, that's not so surprising. The oracle was probably stoned most of the time."

Maggie laughed.

"It's true." He smiled. "Delphi sits over a fault line. Gases escape from the earth from an underlying crevasse exactly where the Oracle's tripod used to sit."

"That's so bizarre." She looked around. "You've missed Greece, haven't you?"

"Maybe." He looked away and pointed to the hillside. "Let's sit down over there and eat. I'm hungry."

"You brought lunch? Here?"

"A picnic."

"You're full of surprises today."

They hiked above the ruins and sat down in the shade of the tallest tree in the area, an ancient oak, and Nick drew several packages from his backpack. Gyros and a salad of cucumbers, tomatoes, onions and feta cheese.

Maggie unwrapped her sandwich. "What's your favorite part of Greece?" She took a bite of the spiced lamb meat, fresh tomatoes and onions slathered with a cucumber sauce and encased in a thick slab of pita bread.

"The islands."

"Why?"

"Because you can find one that fits your every mood."

"So…say I want to party?"

"Go to Mykonos."

"Want to bathe in the sun?"

"Naxos. Beaches right out of paradise."

"Hmm." She jabbed some crispy chunks of salad with her fork and her mouth exploded with flavors.

"Want to hike," he went on, "go to Kefallonia. In the mood for lots of people and gorgeous sunsets, Santorini. Hydra's cosmopolitan. Rhodes is full of history. Meteora is for spiritual journeys. Karpathos is for lovers of windmills and music."

She chuckled. "What do windmills have to do with music?"

"I have no idea. It's what I remember. As a kid."

"So you've been to all of the islands."

"Practically. My mother kept a log. It was her goal to visit them all."

"Which one was your favorite?"

He paused, and Maggie noticed how calm he seemed.

The stress was gone from his eyes and his face was already tanned from one day in the sun. Here, in the mountains of Greece, he looked natural. "I'm not sure I have a favorite island," he said.

"Ah, come on. A memory. A feeling. There must be something that stuck with you."

"Maybe Patmos. We went there several times, so I got to know it well. Some friends of my parents own a home there. It's small. There's no airport, so it's a quiet island. There are many beaches, and you can walk to a fabulous one from the main town." He leaned back and seemed to be reliving a fond memory.

"Don't tell me. There was a girl."

"No. No girls." He laughed. "I was too quiet. Didn't date until college."

"College? Then it must've been love at first sight."

"I've never been in love." He glanced back at her, so serious.

"Never?"

"Never."

Strange. Neither had Maggie. Wasn't there supposed to be a first time for everything?

THEY DROVE down Mount Parnassos and into the valley toward Itea. Nick had surprised himself by actually relaxing to some degree and enjoying Delphi, but then, since he'd seen this all before, much of his mood had to do with watching Maggie.

After the Temple of Apollo, they'd gone to the museum where she'd bounced from one exhibit to another, like a kid eyeing candy displays. She'd gone from the Castallian spring to the Marmaria, without tiring. At the Tholos, a fourth century B.C. rotunda, she'd wandered around, murmuring, "I can't believe this. It's so old."

There was no doubt she'd sparked in him a renewed love of this country. He could never again call it home, but maybe he should be coming *back* every once in a while.

Itea, though not as beautiful as the southern coastal towns, held its own charm. They found a *taverna* along the seafront for some refreshments and some of the best grilled fresh fish he'd ever eaten, then hit a row of tourist shops.

Maggie made a purchase in a tiny jewelry shop. "Evil eyes," she pronounced, dangling three silver bracelets decorated with colorful beads. "One for Kate, Shannon and me. Want one?"

"No thanks."

"Keeps away the bad spirits."

He'd need a lot more than a bracelet for that.

After Maggie stepped outside to glance through some postcards, he found a silver necklace with one simple charm that matched her bracelet. "I'll take this," he said to the clerk, handed over some euros, and joined Maggie on the sidewalk.

"Can you help me put this on?" She held out the bracelet.

He clasped it around her wrist and held out the necklace. "Look what I found."

"It matches!" Her eyes lit up and sparked a warmth inside him. His feelings for Maggie were growing, changing, every day, confusing him. One minute she made him angry, the next he was laughing. Always, what he felt was intense, nothing middle-of-the-road.

He reached behind her, fastened the chain and couldn't resist letting his fingertips brush along her neck. "I wish we had more time," Nick said, faltering. He wished Berk Tarik had never come into his life. "I wish…I were here with you, in Greece, for a different reason."

"Maybe when this project is finished, we can stay for a while."

"I…have something else I have to do." Suddenly, it dawned on him that he should be keeping his distance from Maggie. What if Tarik had followed them here? What if the man was watching right now and Giannis was right?

"Nick—" She grabbed his hand.

"Maggie, it's getting late." He put some distance between them. "We'd better head back to Athens."

"So that's it? It's only midafternoon, and the day's already over?" The disappointment on her face was obvious.

"Well, we could take the long way back." That wouldn't hurt anything. "At Ayíos, we can take a ferry to the Peloponnese, head down the gulf, cross over the Corinth Canal, and have dinner at a quaint place along the waterfront at Elefsina. We can be back in Athens before dark."

"Yeah." She smiled. "What you said."

THEY REACHED the outlying suburbs of Athens very late. Maggie had fallen asleep in the car. Nick parked near their apartment building, opened the passenger door, and nudged Maggie awake. "Hey, we're home." She stirred, barely. "Come on." He helped her out.

Grudgingly, moving like a wet noodle, she wrapped her arm around his waist and shuffled to the apartment door. Nick let them in and helped her down the hall. He nudged open the door to find Kate lying diagonally over the mattress. There was little, if any, space for Maggie.

"Come on, sleepyhead." He took her into his room, got her into the bed, and took off her sandals.

"Where's Kate?" she mumbled, obviously not entirely cognizant.

"Sleeping like a baby, but you're right. She's a bed hog. You're in my room."

"Mmm," she murmured, a lazy smile spreading across her face.

He had to get out of there. Fast.

"Stay with me," Maggie whispered, her eyes closed. "Don't leave." She felt for his hand and held on.

He didn't relish the idea of sleeping on that damned couch. His legs were bound to be aching by morning. Besides, he was dead tired after all that driving and would be out the moment his head hit the pillow. "Okay. Move over." It's not as if anything was going to happen between them.

CHAPTER FOURTEEN

NICK AWOKE with a hard-on that felt the size of a pillar at the Parthenon. No wonder. Maggie was tucked in front of him, his arm flopped over her, his hand under her shirt, his groin right where nature had intended. She'd shrugged out of her shorts during the night, leaving her bottom in only a thong.

She was asleep, her breathing steady and slow. For one blissful moment, he let himself absorb the sensations of having her close. This was Maggie in his arms, fitting perfectly, feeling so right. Why was it, again, that making love to her would be so wrong? Convenient or not, he'd forgotten.

Oh, yeah. Berk Tarik.

Damn. Nick didn't want to remember.

Involuntarily, his hips moved against her soft center. So good. So right. So wrong. He had to stay focused, and he couldn't bring Maggie into this mess. Couldn't let Tarik get to her.

He started to take his hand away. And stopped. Didn't move, didn't breathe. Something had changed. She was awake. Aware. Was it his imagination or was that a peaked and perky nipple he felt against his palm? His erection jumped against her. Slowly, she moved, reached down and cupped him through his boxers. Hard.

"Mmm. We can't do that." He rolled away and onto his back. "What about Kate?"

She reached out and softly closed the door, then turned back, leaned over, and kissed him, a slow, lazy morning kiss. The kind that quickly turns into something much more. Her hands on him, his hands on her, everywhere it seemed, at once. She drew back, a rush of air escaped between her lips. "I've never felt this way before."

"Maggie, stop."

"I can't. You're the only man…"

"You're a virgin? Oh, no." He covered her with the sheet and closed his eyes. Maybe if he didn't look at her. "Go. Definitely go."

"No, I've had sex before, but it was more like something I needed to…"

"Get done? Check off your to-do list?"

"Yeah. I'm not sure if I ever really…ever…"

"Climaxed?" Astonished, Nick opened his eyes again. Ah, she was beautiful. Her face was flush with arousal, her lips kiss-reddened.

"I don't know," she said. "Maybe I have."

"Trust me. You'd know."

How could any man fail so dismally with this woman? Every time they touched, she turned to raw fire in his hands. "I don't get it," he said. "Why haven't you…"

"Kate and Shannon have always been my first priority. The only men in my life have zipped in and out."

"Obviously, in more ways than one," Nick said ruefully, but somehow it made sense to him. Maggie could control things that way.

"It was the way I wanted it." She swung a leg over his hips straddling him. "Until now."

No one was watching. No one had to know. He reached between her legs, pushed aside the thong and touched her, slipped a finger inside her, and the sound that came from her was more whimper than anything.

"Oh, Maggie," he groaned. "You're killing me."

She moved against his erection, nearly taking him inside. "Now," she whispered. "I want to make love to you."

"Whoa, whoa! Too fast." It almost killed him, but he lifted her off. "You can't control everything."

"I like being on top."

"And where has that gotten you?" He smothered her quiet laugh with a kiss and rolled over on top of her, dragging the tangled sheets over them.

"Oh, that's cute." The sarcastic-sounding voice came from the doorway. "Real cute."

Kate? Maggie glanced up in time to see her sister spinning away from the open doorway. "Oh, no." She clambered over Nick and heard him grunt. "Sorry." She grabbed the sheet around her and dashed down the hall. "Kate! That wasn't what it looked like."

"Oh, no?" Kate, fully dressed, crossed her arms. "What did it look like?"

"Like I'd...I was..."

"In bed with a man?"

"Okay." Maggie took a breath, cleared the sleep-induced haze from her brain. "We slept together. We didn't *sleep* together. We didn't *make love*."

"Yet!" Kate went to the door. "Know what, Maggie? I don't care what you do, or who you do it with. I just want you off *my* back." The door slammed behind her.

Feeling completely defeated, Maggie turned around

to find Nick coming down the hallway. "What are we doing?" she asked.

"Nothing at all, Maggie." He started making coffee. "We had a nice day yesterday. We were shot and fell asleep in the same bed. That's all there is to it."

Was it? Why couldn't Maggie shake the feeling that there was so much more going on? Every time she managed to sneak close to him he slammed a door in her face. One of these days she might get her nose broken, and it scared the hell out of her.

KATE STEPPED THROUGH the back door of the studio and into the alleyway for some fresh air. She'd been hunched over the wheel for several long hours and had the kink in her neck to prove it. At the sight of a man casually leaning against the opposite wall, partially hidden in the shadows, she faltered.

"Hello, Kate." He stepped into the light. "I brought you some lunch." It was her new agora friend from the other night.

"What are you doing here?"

"I knew you'd be working hard, so…" He held out a paper bag. "A salad and some *souvlaki*, pork shish-kebabs."

He'd seemed decent, tended to ask a lot of questions for a guy, but never about anything too personal. Showing up here, on the other hand, was stalker-like creepy. "That's okay. I'm not very hungry." She stepped back. "I need to get more work done."

"Kate, wait," he said, adjusting his dark sunglasses. "I'd hope it wouldn't come to this, but I haven't been completely honest with you." He reached inside his jacket, drew out a leather bifold, and displayed a photo ID type badge. "I'm really a detective with the Athens police."

When he started to put it away, Kate quickly said, "Can I see that?"

"Sure." Shrugging, he handed over his identification.

As far as Kate could tell it looked official enough, but then she couldn't read a word of Greek. "I can get IDs off the Internet for a couple bucks. How do I know this one's real?"

"We could go to my station. You could call my department. I only want to ask a few questions. About Nick Ballos."

"What about Nick?"

"How long have you known him?"

"A few weeks."

"He's working for your sister, correct?"

"Yes."

"What does he do for her?"

"Other than sleep with her?" Kate rolled her eyes, still pissed.

"So they are intimate?"

"No. I don't know. Look, what's this all about?"

"Mr. Ballos left Greece five years ago under some...unsavory circumstances. His passport generated a warning notice when he came back into the country, and we're inquiring as to his purpose in Athens. He's wanted for questioning in a murder."

What? Nick? "Is he a suspect?"

"He's a person of interest, as your police would say." This guy had to be lying. Kate might not know Nick all that well, but she knew there was no way Maggie would have Nick around if he wasn't trustworthy. The man went on to ask a number of seemingly inane questions until he came back to Maggie. "What is Nick's relationship with your sister?"

Kate straightened. "I don't think that's any of your business."

"Are they romantically involved?"

She looked away.

"I'll take that as a yes."

"You can take it any way you want, but without some kind of a warrant, I'm finished answering your questions." She turned.

"Kate." He grabbed her arm. "It would be best for everyone involved, especially your sister, if you say nothing of our conversation."

ACCESS DENIED.

Nick smacked the countertop. "Come on!" He stared at the computer screen and resisted the urge to fling his laptop across the room. Dragging his hands through his hair, he closed his eyes as something very close to despair rushed through him.

As if his life had been on hold since Yanni had died, he'd sat for five years on pins and needles, waiting for the perfect moment to set everything right. Now the time was at hand and all he wanted was for this to be over. Done with. For the first time, Nick resented being Yanni's keeper, felt as if a ball and chain hung heavy around his neck. He could step away, let it go. No one would blame him. His mother and father, Kyrena, Angelo. They all thought he was crazy.

Step away.

No. Never. Taking a deep breath, Nick pushed the treacherous thoughts from his mind. A man's honor was never a burden. It was as much a part of him as skin and bones. Right now, Nick wasn't whole, as if the explosion that had killed Yanni had also blown away a part of Nick and now he had to build it back. The sooner he got this business with Berk Tarik and whoever hired the man over and done with, the better. For him. For Maggie. And until this was resolved, he had to quit messing with her.

He refocused on his computer screen. Maggie would soon be back from her errands. If he didn't hurry, he'd miss yet another opportunity to hack into the government's classified files. He concentrated, studied his notes one more time. Everything had been entered verbatim. And still he'd been kicked off the system. "What am I doing wrong?"

"That depends on what you're trying to do."

Dammit. Maggie stood in the apartment doorway. Nick closed down the program and sat back in his chair.

"Can I help?" She walked over and took one look at the blank screen before scanning the notes lying next to him. Over the past several days he'd secretly gathered detailed log-in information, old passwords, names and dates from the department in charge of Yanni's case. She picked up the pad of paper, read what was there, and then tossed it down. "Why are you trying to get into a top-level clearance system? This has nothing to do with our project."

How could he tell her? What could he say that would make her understand?

"Nick?"

There was nothing to say. He'd lied. He'd used her and her company. He'd justified it in his own mind. When he looked at her face, though, all his reasons seemed contrived.

At first, she looked confused, then plain blindsided. "I should have known." She shook her head. "But I guess I didn't want to."

"Maggie—"

"Don't even." She grabbed his laptop and typed in the first few log-in commands he'd written down in his notes.

"What are you doing?"

She ignored him, kept typing. Retyping. It took her a few attempts, but within minutes, she'd hacked into the files he'd been trying to get at for days. Dumbfounded, he stared at the screen as the system booted up. "How'd you do that?"

"Their maintenance guy changes his passwords every Monday. He takes the date and adds one of his kids' names. Figure out which kid. And bingo." She stood back, folded her arms over her chest. "You're in. Go ahead. Do what you're going to do."

"I'm looking for information, Maggie. That's all."

"Whatever."

She turned away.

He reached for her. "Maggie, wait—"

"Don't." She jumped back and glared at him. "I should never have trusted you. I figured you were using my company to get over here and under someone's radar, but I thought, for the most part, you were pretty honest. A man who said exactly what was on his mind. A man without a facade."

"Don't I get a chance to explain?"

"What's the point, Nick? You used me. You used my company. The reason doesn't matter." She headed for the door.

"Yanni wasn't killed in a car accident five years ago," Nick said to her back. She stopped. "Someone planted a bomb in his car. A young husband. A father of two children. He didn't have a chance, and it wasn't a terrorist. It wasn't an accident. It wasn't being in the wrong place at the wrong time. Someone murdered him."

She bent her head, thinking.

He shouldn't care what she thought. He had what he needed. She'd gotten him into the system. But he did care. He wanted her to understand. "I was there when it happened, Maggie. He was looking right at me through the window when the car exploded. By the time the emergency vehicles got there to put out the fire, there was nothing left of him. He was my best, my only friend. My brother." He swallowed past his tightening throat. "There was nothing I could do to stop it."

"So that's how you got the scars."

He nodded.

"They never found his killer?"

Nick shook his head. "No."

"So when you find Yanni's killer you're not turning anything over to the police. Are you?"

Nick turned away.

"You're going to kill him?"

"I owe it to Yanni."

"Nick, you can't do that."

Yes, he could and would.

"You could get killed yourself. Go to prison. Give all you've got to the police, then let it go."

"Like you've let your mom's expectations go?"

"It's not the same thing. Nick, you could die."

He straightened his shoulders. "There's an old saying, only blood will wash away the stain that taints a man's honor. And without honor, Maggie—" his features grew cold as stone "—a man is nothing."

"You're so wrong."

"Imagine if it hadn't been cancer that had killed your mom. What if someone had murdered her? Worse, what if you knew the man who'd done it, and he'd never gotten caught? What if, right now, he was walking around free this very minute. Laughing, dancing, eating in restaurants, enjoying life." Nick paused. "What would you do then, Maggie?"

She put her head down. When she looked back at him, there were tears in her eyes. "You're off my job, Nick."

That wasn't what he'd expected. "I understand."

"And as soon as you've found what you're looking for in those files," she said, pointing at his laptop, "I want you out of this apartment."

"I get it."

"Today."

"I said, I get it!" Nick went back to his screen and ignored the sound of the apartment door closing behind him. She was gone, out of his life. Good. She'd done the right thing and taken care of herself and her company. That was the best possible solution for everyone involved.

Why was it then, that he wanted nothing more than to run after her, apologize, tell her he would drop everything if she would stay? If she'd let him stay. Ignoring the urge to follow Maggie, he forced himself to sit in the chair and search for Yanni's files.

There they were, popping onto the screen, what he'd been waiting for. There didn't look to be anything unusual or spectacular in the information. All the same, he printed off everything. Next, he searched the files for anything on Dimitri Gavras and Berk Tarik. The investigators had found bank accounts and tracked the flow of funds. Transfers had been made into Tarik's account via various computers in Greece's governmental units, including the Department of Public Order.

What? Nick couldn't believe what he was reading.

Could someone in Giannis's department have wanted Yanni dead? The possibilities and the reasons why they didn't make any sense clicked through his mind, one after another. Bottom line? The person who had hired Tarik either worked for the Greek government or had access to their computers. He read on to find they'd attempted to track Stephano's whereabouts on the dates of the transfers and located him on several security tapes in various governmental buildings. But the evidence was circumstantial.

Nick reached for his cell phone, started to dial Giannis's number, and stopped. As much as he wanted to talk to Giannis, he couldn't. What if this old family friend was protecting Stephano for some reason? He needed time to think, to study this information, and Maggie's apartment wasn't the place.

While the printer chugged away, Nick packed his things. He hadn't guessed this would be so hard, but with every shirt he threw in his suitcase, he felt himself moving further and further away from Maggie. What had he expected when he'd started this ball rolling only a few weeks ago?

One thing was for sure, he hadn't counted on caring about Maggie. Or Kate. He hadn't thought about what would happen if he actually lived after confronting Berk Tarik.

For the first time in a long while, Nick thought about the future. He thought beyond Berk Tarik and the man who had hired him, and he realized with a sinking feeling that he didn't only want this business to be over and done with. He wanted to still be alive afterward. He wanted Maggie, her touch, her voice, her smile. For so long he'd been going through the motions in his life, existing day by day. Now, he wanted something more. He wanted what Yanni had made for himself. He wanted a life.

But he could never have one until he dealt with Yanni's killers. He had to get back on track. Whether or not Maggie was standing in the way.

He closed his suitcase, drew the Heart of Artemis pendant and chain out of his pocket, and left it on the kitchen counter. It belonged to Maggie. Whether she knew it or not, he had to admit the truth to himself. She was the closest he'd ever come to giving his heart to a woman.

CHAPTER FIFTEEN

MAGGIE RAN OUT of the apartment building and into the bright midday sun, not knowing what to do, who to talk to. She spun to her right and walked down the sidewalk, putting one foot in front of the other, not really caring where she was going, glancing at the storefronts, but not really seeing the displays. Nothing seemed to matter anymore.

So what if her company was reaching a new level of success and her job was taking off like a rocket? She wasn't sure she enjoyed what she was doing, and her personal life was a mess. She and Shannon would be fine, but Kate? This internship thing had been the last straw. Their relationship would never be the same. More important, she'd fallen in love for the first time with the absolutely wrong man.

Yep, she'd fallen in love. What could these feelings be except love? What else could hurt this much?

The look in Nick's eyes had frightened her. The way he spoke of honor made her wonder if she could ever really understand this man. While he hadn't exactly lied, he hadn't told her the whole truth, either. Worse, he hadn't trusted her, hadn't let her in, hadn't let her help until she was the only one who *could* help. She felt used. Cheap and unimportant. And unloved. She was in love with a man who didn't love her back.

Maggie passed the patisserie she'd been frequenting and, not the slightest bit hungry, kept walking. She stopped for the light at the crosswalk. People crowded in around her, waiting, brushing her arms. The light turned and her feet, on automatic pilot, moved again.

A liquor store, a coffee shop, a tourist trap, an art studio. Maggie stopped and glanced at the window display. The glazes, dramatic black on yellow, were different from anything Maggie had ever seen, but the designs looked familiar. A contemporary twist on classic Greek pottery.

This was Kate's work.

Maggie shaded her eyes, hoping to see farther into the shop. There Kate was, explaining something with her hands to people who probably didn't speak much English. Finally, her sister brought a piece of pottery toward the front. She stopped when she saw Maggie, faltered, and then went on to set the large vase beside the rest of her display.

Maggie went inside. "Hi."

"Hey."

"These are beautiful," Maggie said. "So different from what you've done before, but I could tell they were yours."

"Really?" Kate asked, uncertain and insecure.

"Really." Maggie bit her lip. This was it. She had to try one last time. "But Mom wanted you to go to college."

Kate glanced up at her, tears in her eyes. "You know, I barely remember her. But in the images I do have she's always happy. Laughing, smiling, hugging us. I have to believe, Maggie, that more than anything, Mom would want me to be happy."

Mom, a little help here. Happy, yes? College, no?

Yeah, their mother would've wanted them all to be happy. *After* college. Maggie smiled to herself. But that's because she believed education was the way to happiness. Only because she hadn't had an opportunity to get one herself. Kate's opportunities for college weren't just here today. They'd be there for her tomorrow, too. Especially with this internship on her resume.

"No more drinking," Maggie said.

"It won't happen again. That was stupid. I was mad at you."

Oh, Kate. Maggie felt so inadequate. All this time, she should have been supporting her sister and her dream, helping her make it come true, instead of pummeling that very dream down at every opportunity. "Kate, I'm sorry. I was wrong. You deserve a shot at making your dreams come true."

Tears spilled down Kate's cheeks. Without a word, she walked over to Maggie and hugged her tight and tighter still.

"We need to get you home soon." Maggie drew back. "So you're back in time for that internship with Rufus."

Kate nodded, too emotional for words.

"Do you want to go now? Today?"

She nodded again. "I helped this guy with his orders, now I want to go home."

Maggie waited while Kate explained the situation to the owner. Apparently, he tried talking her into staying. Kate remained firm. The potter paid her for her work, and Maggie and Kate went outside.

"Oh, my God!" Kate said, turning to Maggie the moment the hot sun hit the tops of their heads. "I almost forgot."

"What?"

"The cop."

"What cop?"

"This guy," Kate went on. "Said Nick is wanted for questioning in a murder."

"Hold on. Start from the beginning. When did you meet him?"

Kate's eyes flashed this way and that. "He's probably watching us. We need to get home." She explained everything as they hurried back to the apartment.

"I don't know what's going on," Maggie said, the moment she shut the door behind them. "Nick's not hiding from anyone. The police could've brought him in any time they wanted. What did this guy look like?"

"Dark hair, tan, wide forehead." Kate grabbed her hair and pulled it back. "He had a...you know..."

"A receding hairline?"

"Yeah."

The grainy photo of that man she'd spotted on Nick's computer back at her office in D.C. popped into Maggie's mind. She went to her laptop and opened the file. "Is this the guy?"

Kate glanced at the photo. "Yep. That's him."

"We need to tell Nick."

"Where is he?" Kate glanced around. "His stuff is gone."

"I kicked him out," Maggie said.

"No shit?"

Maggie paced the floor, explaining.

"I get it," Kate said.

"Do you? 'Cause I don't." She sat at the counter and spotted the gold necklace. No note. Nothing. She picked it up and squeezed it in her hand. Had he left it here on purpose or by accident?

"What is that?"

She let it dangle from her fingers. "The Heart of Artemis."

"That fake cop asked if you two were…were involved."

"This is really creepy."

"What do we do? Go to the Athens police?"

"No." Maggie tightened her grip on the pendant. "I'm calling Nick." She flipped open her cell phone. "Go pack. I'm getting you out of here. Today. You're going home."

"What if Nick… I don't want you getting into trouble."

"Nick hasn't done anything wrong, okay? As mad as I am with him right now, I…" She glanced at Kate, did her best to separate the lies from the truth. She thought about the way Nick had looked at her, how he'd kissed her, touched her.

"He would never hurt us," Maggie said. "I know I can trust him. With my life. And yours." This was all getting too real. As Maggie dialed his cell number, she felt herself sway and grabbed the countertop.

"Maggie?" Kate said, reaching for her arm. "You okay?"

She turned around to find Kate's eyes filled with concern. When had her little sister's face gotten so mature, so caring? "I'm scared. I don't know what's going on, and I'm sorry for putting you in danger."

"Hey, this is more excitement than I've had my entire life." Kate smiled.

"I'm scared for Nick, too." She was more than scared for him. So much more.

The key to life was love.

She studied the necklace. That's when it dawned on

her. The pendant was a puzzle. Maggie held it in her palm and shifted the sides of the little box. They came undone, one after another. As she straightened them, re-aligning them along a tiny hinge to form a small key with the little heart dangling from the shaft, the truth stared back at her.

Oh, hell. It was as clear to her as that little heart dangling in her hand. She'd fallen in love with Nick. Recklessly. Desperately. Completely.

Like it or not, he was the key to her life.

THE TAXI SCREECHED to a halt outside Maggie's apartment. "Here," Nick said to the driver, handing him a handful of euros. "Five minutes. There's more if you're still waiting."

Nick fingered the cold butt of the 9mm Glock holstered under his suit coat, ran into the building, and double-timed it up the steps. He knocked on their door. "Maggie, it's me." The chain slipped off the lock, and the door opened.

She looked scared, and Giannis's comments about the fate of Tarik's innocent victims came back to him in surround sound. Nick brushed the back of his knuckles against her cheek and noticed he was trembling. If only he had time, time to tell her what she'd come to mean to him, time to spend one more night holding her, time to make love. Once.

"What's going on?" she asked.

He shut the door behind him and reset the chain. "I've gotten you involved in something very dangerous, and though that wasn't my intent, Maggie, I'm sorry. For now, we need to concentrate on getting you and Kate safe. That means out of Greece. Fast." He glanced at Kate. She looked shell-shocked. "It'll be okay, honey. You and Maggie will be home before you know it."

"Are you coming?" Maggie asked.

"If I do, then they'll only come after us. It's me they want, so you and Kate need to get out of the picture. You packed?"

"Kate's ready. But I'm in the middle of this project for Giannis. I can't leave."

"Yes, you can." He strode down the hall and threw her belongings into her suitcase. "I called Alex. The A-Team can deal without you. They've got everything under control."

"You...called Alex, without consulting me?"

"This isn't a game, Maggie." He slammed her suitcase shut and walked back down the hall with her trailing behind. "You and Kate are in this because of me. This is the only way I know to get you out of this." He grabbed Kate's suitcase. "Let's go."

MAGGIE SAT IN THE TAXI, telling herself over and over, *It'll be okay. It'll be okay.* She wasn't worried for herself, only for Kate. As soon as her sister was on that flight out of here, Maggie would calm down.

Nick directed the taxi driver toward the front of a jeweler's shop nestled between an electronics store and some kind of deli. It was the place she'd followed him to last week. With all that had passed since then, that day felt as if it'd been a year ago.

"I thought we were going to the airport. Why are we stopping here?"

"I have to get something. Five more minutes," he told the driver. "Kate and Maggie. Come on, I don't want you two waiting out here."

Maggie followed Kate out of the cab. Nick slipped his hand possessively under Maggie's elbow and drew her across the sidewalk. He looked behind her for a moment, then opened the door to the jeweler's shop.

The door hadn't closed behind them before a skinny Greek man glanced up from a tray of watches. He quickly referred the customer he'd been working with to his assistant, then came from the other side of the glass counter to meet them, gap-toothed grin brightening his otherwise dark, leathery complexion.

"Well, Nick, what did I do to deserve these two gorgeous visitors?" The man kissed Nick on each cheek before Nick made introductions. "Hello, Miss Kate and Miss Maggie." The man's grin grew wider as he shook Maggie's hand and held on. "You have lovely, long fingers. Perhaps I could interest you in a selection of rings—"

"I don't think—" Maggie hesitated.

"We don't have time, Angelo," Nick said. "This situation is messier than I expected. To be safe, can I borrow one of your men for a few weeks, until this situation is resolved."

"Why?" Angelo's smile disappeared. "What's happened?"

"Tarik's made contact with Kate. I need to get these two out of here. Now."

"Say no more." Angelo glanced over Maggie's head. "Riley?"

Maggie spun around to find two guards, men she hadn't noticed, they'd been so still and quiet, near the door.

"I'm on it." The man who stepped forward was obviously American, as big as a truck and as buff as a soldier. "Tell me what you want me to do."

"Maggie and Kate, this is Riley." Angelo introduced them. "He's been with your military for many years. Last year, I saved his life in Egypt. Now, he feels as if he owes me." He turned to the bodyguard. "Protect them with your life, and, when this is done, please consider your debt to me as paid. Do whatever Nick says." Riley nodded.

"Thank you," Nick said, hugging Angelo. "I owe you."

"Stay safe," Angelo said. "All of you."

"Let's go." Riley headed outside and studied the street and the upper levels of the buildings. "We're clear." He signaled for them to follow. Instead of making Maggie feel safer, all this cloak-and-dagger business was only making her more frightened.

Nick grabbed her hand and pulled her along with him back into the waiting taxi. "I want you and Kate on the next flight out of Athens," he said. "I don't care where it's headed."

CHAPTER SIXTEEN

"I'M NOT GOING!" For added measure, Maggie grabbed onto the inside door handle of the taxi. "This project is far too important for me to risk losing it." She hated the thought of Kate heading out alone, but once her sister was on that plane she'd be safely out of this mess.

Nick stood on the sidewalk in front of the Athens airport, holding open the rear taxi door. "Dammit, Maggie! You won't lose this job. Get out of the cab!"

"No." She glanced out at Kate, then at Riley. He was definitely on high alert. No one was getting to her sister through that brick wall. "Alex has never managed a team before," she explained. "He has crappy organizational skills."

"Give it a rest, Nick," Kate said. "I don't need Maggie to come along. I'm going alone. Besides," she said, waving a thumb at Riley. "I've got Tarzan here."

Riley's concentration didn't waver from the surroundings. The only indication he'd heard Kate's flippant comment was a slight thinning of his lips.

Nick took another long look at the travelers and airport personnel surrounding them, then jumped back into the rear seat of the taxi. He handed the driver some money and jerked his head toward the sidewalk. The driver shrugged and climbed out of the vehicle, slamming the door behind him.

"Maggie." Nick turned back to her. There was no doubt his badly worn patience was close to being nonexistent. Too bad. Maggie got to decide where she was going and when. "Are you really going to let Kate leave here alone?"

Guilt trip. Big time. "You know as well as I do," she said, lowering her voice so only he could hear, "that if someone managed to get through Riley there'd be nothing—nothing—I could do to stop it."

"Look. This problem disappears for you when you leave this country," Nick argued. "There's no reason for them to follow you and Kate."

See? She was right. Kate would be fine.

"This problem follows me wherever I go," he went on, "unless I choose to disappear, and I won't do that. There's something I need to do. I'm not leaving Athens until it's done." He closed his eyes. "I don't expect you to understand."

"Understand what?" Her voice cracked, tears stung the back of her throat. "If this is more crap about blood for honor, I don't want to hear it."

"Dammit, Maggie!" He slammed his fist into the driver's headrest. "I'm staying! You're going! If I have to drag you all the way down to the terminal. Get out of the taxi!"

She'd never seen anyone look quite so angry, or so dangerous. His eyes flashed, his nostrils flared. The knuckles on his fist were white with restraint. Still, she wasn't frightened of *him*. She was only frightened by the possibility of losing him.

When push came to shove, she didn't really give a damn about this Greek contract. "Agree to come along," she said. "And I'll consider getting on a plane." She had to try, at least.

"Arrgh!" He rested his head in his palms, rubbing at his eyes. "I'm going to see when the next flight to somewhere safe leaves. It's not a good idea for you to be alone right now. Will you please come with me?"

"Not without your promise that you'll fly out of here with me."

He took one long look at her, then studied their surroundings. "Don't you take one step out of this taxi before I get back." He jumped back onto the sidewalk and said to Riley, "Let's get you guys on a flight out of here."

"Kate!" Maggie yelled.

Kate stuck her head inside the cab.

"When you get home, stay at Shannon's. Just to be sure."

"Right."

"I don't know if I'll make it to your exhibition. Knock 'em dead, okay?"

Kate nodded, her lips trembling. "I love you, Maggie."

"I love you, too." Maggie squeezed her sister's hand, then watched as she disappeared into the terminal.

ANNOYED, FRUSTRATED, AND YES, fearful for the first time in this whole deal, not for his sake but for Maggie and Kate's, Nick stalked through the terminal. He went to the first available airline attendant and bought three tickets to the next available flight out of Greece.

When he ran back to Kate and Riley, he handed two tickets to Kate. "Better get through customs and security. ASAP. You leave in two hours for Paris, then on to D.C. from there."

"Thanks." She took the tickets. Then she surprised

the hell out of him by dropping her suitcase and lunging at him. Though Kate looked, for all intents and purposes, like an adult, her arms around him felt like a young girl's. He hugged back, and Riley discreetly turned away, giving them privacy. "It'll be okay."

"Take care of her," Kate said, her voice breaking.

"She's getting on the plane, if it's the last thing I do."

"No, she won't. She's using the project here as an excuse to stay with you. She loves you."

Dammit. Nick stared at Kate. That was the last thing he wanted to hear. "She shouldn't."

"Shouldn't?" Kate laughed. "Maybe I *shouldn't* love to throw pots. Maybe my mom shouldn't have died."

"That's different. That's something you had no control over."

"You think love is something to be controlled?"

"You can't love someone if you don't let yourself."

"That must be what you're doing, then, not letting yourself."

Nick looked away.

"You think, for one second," Kate said, "that if Maggie could control this, she wouldn't? We're talking about someone who set my bedtime for me until I was sixteen. Trust me, if Maggie could control her feelings for you, she'd stop loving you in a heartbeat."

"What the hell does that mean?"

"Ha!" Kate shook her head. "Doesn't sound like real love, does it? If you could shut it off and on."

"Once this is all over, things will be different."

"Yeah, from the sounds of it, you'll either be in jail or dead."

"Enough!" Nick turned. "Riley, get her on that flight. No matter what."

"You got it."

"Goodbye, Kate."

"Nice knowing ya," Kate whispered.

MAGGIE WATCHED THE TERMINAL door for Nick. Seconds seemed to take minutes, minutes clicked by like hours. The rear taxi door suddenly swung open and a man she'd never met before climbed inside. She lunged for the other door when he clamped his hand over her mouth, grabbed her arm and yanked her back against him.

"Shh, Miss Maggie. Angelo Bebel sent me to warn you. There was someone following you and Mr. Ballos."

Maggie stiffened against the man's hold.

"You'll be safe with me," he said, letting his hand fall away.

"How do I know Angelo sent you?"

"He decided one guard wasn't enough." He glanced quickly around. "Come. We must find a safer place for you."

"Nick said to wait here. I'm not going anywhere without him."

His grip tightened, and she braced herself for the tug she felt certain would come. Surprisingly, they stayed rooted to the seat. The man had spotted something near the terminal. She looked up to find Nick walking slowly, purposefully toward them, his gaze intent on the man next to her in the backseat of the taxi. The car door swung open and Nick leaned inside. "Sir, I think you have the wrong cab."

"Mr. Ballos," the man said. "Angelo sent me. Along with his own car for you and Miss Dillon." The man motioned behind him with his head. "Behind us."

The driver who'd brought them to the airport and

whose taxi they were sitting in walked over to Nick and said, "Are we going, or what?"

"Give us a minute." After the man walked away, Nick stuck his head back inside the vehicle. "As soon as I get Maggie on her flight, I'll join you. You have my word." His voice sounded too tight, too controlled.

Something was very wrong. She tried sliding across the seat away from the man, and his grip tightened.

"We *will* be leaving in that car, Mr. Ballos," the man holding Maggie said. "Or Miss Dillon here will not be happy."

"Leave her out of this," Nick said. "I'll go with you. Alone."

"Those are not my orders."

Maggie's heart all but stopped at the feel of hard, cold metal through the lightweight fabric of her sundress.

"Does he have a gun, Maggie?" Nick asked quietly, never taking his eyes off the man.

"It…it feels like it could be. Against my back."

The man climbed out of the taxi, dragging Maggie after him. He jerked his head toward a gray sedan. "Move! Now!"

Another stranger jumped out of the driver's seat of the sedan. He pushed Nick into the front and opened the back door. The man shoved Maggie into the car, climbed in after her, and they sped away. They drove toward Athens. After a short time, the driver pulled into an industrialized area and stopped on a completely deserted street. The driver jumped out and, pointing some kind of automatic rifle at Nick, ordered him out of the car. The man in the back dragged Maggie out after him.

Nick stood calmly on the sidewalk, but Maggie

noticed the tension in his stance. He spoke quietly. "I'm asking you again to leave Maggie out of this."

Both of the men ignored Nick, directing Maggie and Nick into a partially demolished building. Someone pushed her ahead of Nick through dark, dusty halls.

"She has nothing to do with this," Nick continued. "Let her go."

"I can't do that, Ballos." The man who'd climbed into their taxi at the airport brought them to a stop in the near center of a cavernous room. "The deal was for both of you."

Nick turned back. "Name your price, then, for her to get on a plane and fly out of here unharmed."

"Tempting. Unfortunately, I've never known a dead man to make good on his debts."

The driver set down his gun and tied Nick's hands. He seemed nervous and inexperienced. Maggie saw Nick clench his fists, trying to create extra space. Maggie watched, waited for him to make a move.

"Take us to a bank," Nick said, after the man had finished tying him. "I can have a million dollars wired in today."

"Shut up," the man muttered.

"You can have it put in any account." Nick continued. Maggie could see him working his hands out of the bindings. "Anywhere you want. All you have to do is leave Maggie out of this."

"I said shut up!" The man lifted his hand.

"No!" she screamed as the man slammed the butt of his gun against Nick's head. Dodging the driver, she reached for Nick's slumping form. She was next, guessed it an instant before pain ripped through her skull.

THROBBING. One hundred bass drums pounded at once inside his head. Nick had fallen, or been thrown, on his stomach, his hands bound behind him. He couldn't have been out for more than a few minutes, but the thickness in his head made it feel as if he'd been out for hours. Chunks of cement rubble dug into his cheeks. Dust and sand covered his lips, filled his nostrils. And his throat was dry, so dr—Maggie!

He jerked his head. The floral print of her skirt came into focus, then swirled into a mass of pastel colors. Her prone form tipped and spun. He closed his eyes, willing his equilibrium to return.

"Maggie?" His voice cracked in the silence. He opened his eyes again. Oh, God! She wasn't moving. He focused on the dark stream of dried blood angling down her temple and cheekbone. This was his fault. His fault.

Footsteps crunched across the ground and stopped beside him. "Get up." That was the voice of the man who had climbed into the taxi back at the airport. "I said move!"

A booted foot sunk into his side. With his hands tied, Nick doubled up on the ground, trying to protect himself as kick after kick landed, first in his stomach, then his side, then his chest.

"Stop." A voice unfamiliar to Nick sounded quietly from a short distance away. "The deal was for him alive."

The man stepped away. Nick took a deep breath, dragged himself to his knees, and inched toward Maggie. He nudged her side with his knee. "Maggie. Maggie?" She didn't stir, but her chest moved slowly up and down.

"She's all right...for now," the quiet voice sounded again.

Nick turned his head toward the sound, and the distorted, surreal face of the man who had plagued Nick's nights for years came to life before him. Berk Tarik. A rush of blood flooded his head. The air left his lungs.

"I understand you've been looking for me." Tarik smiled. "Tell me, what were you planning to do once you found me?"

"Untie my hands and you'll find out."

Tarik chuckled. "I assume this to be a vendetta of some sort. You'll have to refresh my memory."

"Five years ago. Yanni Kythos."

"Ahh. Now this makes sense." Tarik nodded several times. "It's appropriate then, that you and I should meet. Your friend was my first assignment. You two will be my last."

"I thought Stephano's deal was for us to be handed over alive," he said, fishing.

Tarik laughed.

"You're going to kill me anyway," Nick argued. "You might as well tell me the truth. Did Stephano hire you?"

Tarik studied him and then, very slowly, nodded.

Nick couldn't believe it. A vibrant wave of nausea passed through him and was quickly followed by an anger more intense and vile than anything he'd ever felt. His hands shook, his face heated. He couldn't think past the desire to find Stephano and kill the man with his bare hands.

Maggie moaned, and all thoughts of vengeance fled Nick's mind. She'd opened her eyes and tentatively lifted her head. Then she sat up, obviously too abruptly, and stopped, holding her head in her hands, bracing herself against his side. "Nick," she murmured.

Stephano and Tarik be damned. If only he could put his arm around her and brush back the tangle of auburn curls falling across her ashen face. If only he could tell her everything was going to be all right.

He'd screwed up so badly. The only thing that mattered now was getting her out of here. Slowly, he tested the tension in the bindings around his wrist. Tight as a drum. Someone must have retied the knots while he was out cold.

Quickly, he surveyed their surroundings and Tarik's manpower. They were still in the same building situated at the outskirts of the city. The roof was entirely gone, allowing for no shade from the scorching midafternoon sun. The interior had been largely destroyed, leaving little hope for finding cover other than a stand of cement pilings twenty feet to the left. His Glock was lying on top of the pilings.

Their only saving grace was the muted sound of traffic filtering in through the crumbling window frames. If they were able to escape, help wouldn't be far away.

There were three men. Only Tarik was unarmed. Tarik and the man who'd climbed into the cab with Maggie were both Nick's match physically and appeared maliciously confident. The driver of the car, on the other hand, was wiry and short, apparently uncertain about his involvement in this escapade. He was the weak link, if only Maggie would become lucid enough to cooperate. Her free hands were the only thing between them and sure death. For now, he had to stall.

"If it's money you're after, Tarik, I can double what Stephano offered you. Set us free, tell Stephano we escaped, and that will be the end of it."

"There he goes again," the man muttered and kicked Nick in the gut.

"No!" Maggie screamed and scuttled in front of

Nick, shielding him from another kick, holding her arms about him to keep him from falling on his face.

"Wait. I want to hear what he has to say." Tarik calmly held out his hand toward the other man. "How much are your lives worth to you?"

Nick strained his wrists against the ropes, then stopped, calming himself, taking the comment for what it was worth—confirmation that the plan was to kill Maggie as well. He had to keep his wits about him if he was going to get her out of this alive. He leaned over on his way to standing and whispered in her ear, "We'll get out of this. Stay alert."

Once on his feet, he limped toward Tarik, stopping a few feet away. "Name your price. I can have the money wired anywhere today, under the condition that Maggie and I remain unharmed."

"Unharmed? Unharmed." Tarik paced, rubbed his chin back and forth. "Mahmud." He jerked his head toward Nick. The hired gun immediately strode across the sandy floor. Slinging his automatic rifle over his shoulder, he gripped Nick's arms, holding him back. Tarik stopped in front of Maggie and nodded toward the driver. The man set his weapon on a cement slab behind him and yanked Maggie to her feet, pulling her arms behind her back.

Tarik studied Maggie. "You know, Ballos, this woman of yours is…very passionate," he said softly, touching his finger against the dark streak of dried blood trailing across her cheek.

A sick, helpless feeling curled in Nick's gut, then wound itself into a rage. Suddenly, he was no longer himself. A monster had taken over his body and mind. He barely felt the rough cords drawing fresh blood at his wrists as tension surged through his muscles and he struggled against the man's restraining hold. The man Tarik had called Mahmud pulled roughly back against Nick's arms, sending jolts of pain across his shoulders and back.

"Wanting your hands loose from that rope, eh, Ballos? Think again."

The deep-throated chuckle sounding near Nick's ear finally snapped him out of his deranged state. An opportunity for escape was slipping away.

He took a good, measuring look at Maggie. She was holding her chin high, her shoulders square, staring Tarik down as if she were the one with the upper hand. Only Nick noticed the slight quiver in her lips. He caught her gaze and held it. She was truly terrified, but at least she'd be ready when he made a move. With a brief glance and nod, he signaled toward the pile of cement slabs. She seemed to understand.

"If you touch her again, Tarik," Nick yelled, "my deal with you is off. Then you can settle for whatever scraps Stephano throws your way."

Tarik threw back his head and laughed. The sound echoed through the hollow skeleton of the building like a war cry. "Hold her still," Tarik ordered the driver, then he crossed over to stand directly in front of Nick and grinned. "I think, Mr. Ballos, you'll make a deal with me as long as this woman is *alive*. No matter her condition."

Nick rammed his knee into Tarik's crotch. Tarik grunted and crumpled. Nick dropped down, quickly levering Mahmud over his shoulder and onto the ground. Mahmud bounced to his feet. He stepped forward, ready to jab the butt of his gun into Nick's head. Shifting to the left, Nick thrust a kick into the other man's side, then another above his knee, forcing

Mahmud to the ground again. It wasn't much, but it gave them the precious few seconds they needed.

The driver still held Maggie. Bewildered, the man watched Nick. When Nick darted toward him, the man let go of Maggie and reached low for his weapon. "Now, Maggie! Run!" Nick slammed his foot into the man's face.

She raced for the cement pilings. Nick snatched the shoulder strap of the driver's gun and ran after her. A stream of shots rang out from behind them. Bullets chinged against cement, creating clouds of dust as Maggie reached for the Glock. A sudden sharp pain sliced through his side. He stumbled, then continued on, sliding behind the safety of the pilings only seconds before another burst of rapid fire disrupted the stillness of the vacant building.

He dropped the gun and fought with the ropes binding his wrists. He bit down against the pain in his side. "Are you all right?"

Breathing hard, she nodded. Bullets flew around them, thudding into the dirt and hitting cement. She was scared, trembling, but unharmed. And she'd managed to grab his Glock.

"Fire a few shots out there to keep them away. Then get the knife from my pocket."

She inched toward the top of the four-foot-tall stand of cement and directed several shots toward Tarik and his men. There was no answering fire. She dug into his pocket, pulled out a small, folded blade, and cut away at the ropes.

"Fire another shot. Quick." This time, they fired back. "Keep your head down!"

She crouched low.

"Cut this damned rope. Hurry, Maggie!"

She fumbled with the knife, managed to mostly cut through before the rope fibers mercifully gave way. Nick grabbed the driver's automatic rifle and glanced over the top of the cement. "I'm in a damn good spot here, Tarik, and you've got nothing," Nick yelled. For good measure he let loose with a few rounds. "I've got two guns, and I can see you coming from any direction. With all this firing going on, it won't be long before the authorities find their way here."

"Unfortunately, Mr. Ballos, you are right," Tarik returned. For a moment, the only sound was crunching sand and cement, then car doors slamming and an engine firing to life.

Maggie glanced toward Nick. "Are they gone?"

"God, I hope so." He rubbed dripping sweat from his forehead, then took a look over the top of the slabs. "Let's go."

"Shouldn't we wait for the police or something?"

"They'd detain us for days. We'd be sitting ducks for Tarik." He made his way through the rubble toward what looked to be the front of the building. After a hundred yards or so, his strength completely deserted him. An intense pain throbbed in his side. He leaned against a wall, felt himself sliding to the ground.

"Nick? There's blood on the wall." She reached under his arms to support him. "Oh, my God! You've been shot!"

CHAPTER SEVENTEEN

MAGGIE KNELT DOWN, stuffing Nick's Glock into the waist of her skirt. Only now did she see the red stain oozing through the dark khaki of his shirt. He was losing too much blood.

Calm. She had to stay calm. He wasn't going to die. She wouldn't let him. "I'm going to unbutton your shirt to see how badly you've been shot."

"It's my…side." His hands fell lax on the ground, and he closed his eyes. "He only nicked me. A few…" he paused, taking slow, short breaths, "stitches, and I'll be all right."

She fumbled with the buttons and gently peeled back the sticky, blood-soaked fabric, barely holding back a gasp at the extent of the wound. She took a deep breath. "If this is a nick, then I'm a damn sight queasier than I thought."

"Let's hope it went in and out. Is the bullet still…in me?"

"I'll check," she whispered, then leaned over him and examined his back. There was no hole going in one side and out the other. The bullet had apparently sliced his side, tearing and spreading the tissue wide. "There's no bullet in you, but you're losing a lot of blood." She pulled off her cotton slip and made a pad wide enough to compress against his wound. Then she ripped off a long thin strip from the bottom of her skirt and tied it around his waist. "That should help, but we have to get you to a hospital."

"No," he murmured. "That's the first place they'll look." He rested his head against the wall. "Angelo's. You...go there. He can send someone to...get me."

"I'm not leaving without you."

He smiled weakly. "That's what got us into this trouble in the first place."

Maggie nearly burst into tears. "Your other side is fine. Get up and lean on me. We have to find a taxi." She grabbed his left hand, flipped it over her shoulder, and hoisted him to his feet. His full weight almost toppled her over until she spread her legs and found her balance.

"Leave me, Maggie. I'll only slow you down."

"Damn you!" she cried. "If you would've listened to me at the airport, we wouldn't be in this mess. You're coming with me, so help out here, okay?"

He shifted himself then and walked slowly alongside her. In minutes and only a few more stumbles, they'd made it out to the sidewalk, into the blinding sunlight. Another block and they'd found a busy street.

"They'll be watching for us." He sounded weak and incredibly tired.

"I know."

Police cars with sirens screaming zoomed down the street and Maggie and Nick acted like a couple, arm in arm. After the last of the police had passed, Maggie quickly leaned Nick against a wall and flagged down a taxi. The driver pulled over to the side of the road and stared uneasily at them. Maggie helped Nick into the cab, then stuffed money in the driver's palm. Nick let his head fall back against the seat and gave the driver Angelo's address.

Although she watched the road behind them, it was impossible to pick out any single vehicle that might be following. "Nick, ask the driver to make a few quick turns."

When he didn't make a sound, her heart tripped in fear. His head had now fallen forward, his eyes were closed and his mouth slack. She felt the inside of his wrist, then relaxed as his slow, steady pulse beat its way through her fingers. He was out. She was on her own.

Fifteen minutes later, she still hadn't discerned whether or not there was a car following them. As they neared the front of Angelo's shop, Maggie grew more uneasy. Earlier in the day, the men that had been at the airport may have followed them from their apartment to Angelo's. That meant they might be watching and waiting for them here.

The driver slowed down the vehicle, and Maggie urged him on by waving her hand forward. "Go! Go!" she said, grasping for the Greek word. "*Pao. Pao! Parakalo.*"

The driver seemed to understand and continued on. Maggie watched the street behind them. There were too many cars. "Turn!" she yelled and pointed at the next intersection. The driver started at her abrupt command, but swung the car to the right. After three more turns, Maggie was certain no one was following them.

"I need to find a market," she said to the driver, hoping he'd understand. He looked at her blankly through the rearview mirror. "Shopping. An a…*agora*!" She made the motions of putting a scarf over her head. "I need a scarf."

"Yes! Yes! *Agora*," he repeated. He drove a few blocks, then took a left. He pulled off to the side of the road and pointed down the alley. "*Kaskol*." He put his hands over his head. "Here."

She glanced down at Nick. The makeshift bandage was completely saturated with blood. Ripping off several more inches of her skirt, she made another, exchanged it for the first one, and tied it tightly. Brushing her fingertips against his cheek, she kissed his forehead and lips. "I'll be back," she whispered against his cheek.

After promising the driver more money on her return, she jumped out of the cab and ran toward the vendor carts. A variety of scarves, shawls, and skirts were displayed at one of the first merchant's stands she passed. With any luck at all and the right clothing, she might be able to pass for an old Greek woman. She bought one of each in a drab brown and a few other supplies and ran down the alley toward Angelo's shop, shrugging on the skirt, pulling on the shawl, and tying the scarf over her head as she went.

When she reached the right street, she forced herself to slow down to a normal walking pace, ignoring the sweat dripping down her back and side of her face. It seemed to take forever to make it to the small shop, but she did it. Casually, she hoped.

She opened the door and stepped inside. Angelo's assistant was working near the front with a harmless-looking customer. He said something incomprehensible to Maggie, then returned to the customer. Maggie walked back toward the rear room of the shop. "Angelo," she whispered.

She heard a chair scrape, then he stepped onto the front sales floor, squinting his eyes suspiciously and moving toward her. "Maggie?"

"We were kidnapped at the airport." She kept her voice lowered. "Nick was shot. He's lost a lot of blood."

He grasped her hand. "Where is he now?"

"In a cab not far from here."

"You are not hurt?"

"I'm fine."

"I was afraid something terrible had happened. Some time ago a car with two men inside stationed itself on the other side of the street. They've been waiting. For you and Nick to return, I assume."

"We need your help—a doctor and someplace safe to stay."

He shook his head. "There is no safe place to stay in Athens. Tarik will be watching everywhere—not only my shop, but my home and my relatives' homes."

"There has to be someplace we can go. He could die if he doesn't get medical attention!"

Angelo quickly scribbled down an address onto a scrap of paper. "Give this to the driver and make sure no one follows you. When you get to the marina, ask for Omar. I will leave the shop in a few minutes and join you as soon as I can."

NICK WAS SO TIRED. He'd never felt this kind of pervasive, bone deep exhaustion. Or this weakness. He attempted lifting his head, but the heavy thing wouldn't cooperate. It probably had something to do with the inviting comfort of whatever his face was resting on. Warm and soft an…hmm, he took a breath.

Maggie. He could smell her, feel her, the outline of her thighs beneath his ear and her stomach against his nose. Her fingertips caressed his forehead and cheek, brushed through his hair. Aahhh. He could stay here an eternity.

"Nick," she whispered, her voice urgent and sharp, directly contradicting the feel of her touch. "We have to get moving, and I need your help."

There was a tinge of fear in her voice, too. It snapped him to alertness. He opened his eyes and rolled from his left side onto his back. The dull ache of bruised muscles and ribs impeded his progress, but it was the sharp pain jolting through his side that completely immobilized him.

It all came back to him in a rush. "Did you lose them?" he grunted, grabbing the top of the backseat and pulling himself into a sitting position.

"Yes."

"You're sure."

"Positive. We've been crisscrossing through the streets for fifteen minutes. I haven't seen anyone on our tail."

Nick kicked open the door, handed the driver some euros, and said, "*Eeseekho.*"

The man nodded, motioned zipping his lips.

"I've already paid him," Maggie said.

"That's a little extra for his silence. I'm not naive enough to think it'll buy more than a few days worth, but every minute's going to count."

Maggie came around to Nick's side of the cab. He balked at the sight of her in old women's clothing. "Very attractive costume."

"I disguised myself before going into Angelo's shop."

"Smart move."

She checked his makeshift bandages again and seemed satisfied that the bleeding had finally stopped. "And this is for you." She threw the blanket she had purchased at the agora around Nick's shoulders to hide his bloodstained shirt.

After thanking the driver profusely, she helped Nick hoist himself out of the car. The moment the door slammed shut, the driver wasted no time in speeding away. Nick glanced around as they walked toward the docks. The sun was setting behind them, casting long shadows over the ground and a purplish glaze over the bay. It was beautiful and serene, but they were out in the open, sitting ducks to Tarik's men if they had, somehow, managed to follow them here.

"What the hell are we doing at a marina?"

"Angelo's going to meet us here. He told me to find a man named Omar."

"The smuggler?" Nick turned his head sharply toward Maggie, then cringed as pain shot down his side. He stopped and leaned more heavily against her. She countered by tightening her grip around him, and he grimaced further.

"Can you make it?"

"I feel great." He forced a smile. "If you discount the fact that I've got a bullet hole in my side, I've lost a couple pints of blood, and my stomach and ribs feel as if someone tenderized me with a rubber mallet."

"Oh, Nick." She rested her forehead against his chest.

For a moment, he let his chin fall to the top of her head. "Let's find Omar's boat and some cover. This marina's making me nervous."

Omar's boat was only a short distance away, a sparkling new fifty-foot cruiser, complete with ample cargo space and high-powered in-board engine, all the trimmings of a successful smuggler. There was no one aboard, so Nick climbed awkwardly over the side and sat down on deck. Maggie sat next to him and yanked a paper bag from her leather satchel.

"Compliments of Angelo." She dug into the bag and pulled out a container of hummus and several pitas, as well as chunks of flaky baklava pastry, and a bottle of water. Suddenly, overcome with emotion, he couldn't find his voice. He could only stare into those full, tawny eyes peering valiantly out at him through folds of heavy brown fabric.

This woman had had one hell of a day. She'd been abducted for something she had inconsequential knowledge of and should have had no part in. She was in a foreign land, spoke little of the language, and, yet, had managed to cart a badly injured man around this huge city for several hours without being discovered. She'd risked her life to save his own sorry ass.

"Maggie." He reached out, ignoring the nagging discomfort from the movement, and drew the scarf from her face. His throat constricted at the sight of her. Her cheeks were tearstained and smudged with dust and grime. That damned streak of dried blood still angled its way down the side of her face, and bruises were beginning to form. Despite all that, she was nothing short of the most beautiful woman he'd ever seen.

"Oh, God, Maggie." He brushed away some of the dirt and rubbed his thumb over her lips. "What have I gotten you into?"

"I was the one who wouldn't leave, remember?"

"You didn't know the full extent of the risks. I'm so sorry. Tarik kidnapped you because he thinks we're lovers."

"I'm only sorry we're not." She burrowed her cheek into his palm. "For one night with you, I'd do anything."

"Then you're a fool."

"No." She covered the back of his hand with her own. "I'm in love." Tears glistened at the corners of her eyes, and her words made him ache to pull her close, to hold her against him. To make the world and all its ugliness go away.

She loved him. The admission had the strangest effect, making him want something, dream of something impossible. Him and Maggie, alone, anywhere. On one of the small barely inhabited Greek isles. Anywhere no one would ever find them. Where a man's honor and duty were unimportant.

Dreams, that's all they were.

Heavy footsteps sounded against the dry wooden dock, shattering his fantasy. He cocked his head and listened. "Four people, maybe more," he whispered. "Maggie, get into the cabin until we know who's here."

She yanked the gun from underneath her robe, and fumbled with the cabin door handle. It wouldn't budge. "It's locked."

"Get behind that captain's chair."

The footsteps stopped beside the boat. Nick ducked his head below the side windows and aimed his Glock toward the dock.

"Nick? Maggie? It's Angelo. I'm here with Omar and my sister."

Nick relaxed and set the gun down. "We're here."

Angelo hoisted Maggie's suitcase on deck and then helped a woman onto the boat, climbed over himself, and knelt by Nick's side. "Are you all right, my friend?"

"I'll live."

"How did you get my things?" Maggie asked.

"I contacted the cab driver at the airport. For a small fortune, he delivered them here." Angelo motioned to the woman waiting patiently behind him. "Tandu, come." While an armed guard maintained position on the dock, Angelo quickly made introductions, explaining that Tandu was his oldest sister and a nurse. Other than her graying hair and slightly less masculine features, she was a mirror image of him, with the same gap-toothed smile and leathery creases near her eyes and mouth.

Although she appeared painfully shy, once she examined Nick's wound, she became direct and sure in her movements.

Nick watched a disgruntled-looking Omar shuffle his huge frame below deck. "Do you think it was wise to meet at a smuggler's boat, Angelo?"

"He's reluctant, yes, but I took a large shipment of jewelry off his hands last month. He owes me and will not talk. Besides, how else were we to quietly get you and Maggie to Patmos?"

"Patmos!" Nick jerked forward and winced as his movement brought Tandu's hand in blunt contact with his mangled flesh. He lay back down and took a deep breath. "I am *not* leaving Athens."

"You're a stubborn man, Nick. Stupid, too."

"I finally have a chance to finish this thing once and for all."

"You have a bullet wound in your side. What can you hope to accomplish other than to endanger Maggie's life again?" Angelo motioned toward Maggie with his out-stretched hand. "I have a home on Patmos. It's easy to guard. Once there, Stamos can protect you and Maggie much longer than I could ever hope to here in the city."

"Take Maggie to the island. I'm staying."

"Bang!" Maggie snapped her fingers. "And I'm out of the picture."

He ignored her, ignored the hurt plainly evident in her eyes and turned toward Angelo. "Tarik wants me. Not her."

"What if I won't go?"

"Dammit, Maggie! We're talking real guns and real assassins."

"Don't you think I know that?" she yelled back at him, then lowered her voice. "*You* get realistic. You're hurt. You're weak. You can't hope to face them in your condition. At least on Patmos, you'd have a chance to recuperate. Besides, I'm not—"

"You're not going without me! Where have I heard that before?"

"Nick!" Angelo interrupted their heated exchange. "Tandu must make several stitches now. Some of them will be inside the wound. She must give you a shot for the pain."

Nick nodded, still glaring at Maggie. He felt the prick of a needle in his arm. In his arm? That wasn't right. If it were something to numb the pain Tandu would have put the shot in his side, by the wound. He threw a questioning glance at Angelo.

"Forgive me, my friend." Angelo bowed his head. "You've given me no other choice."

Nick's entire body grew numb as the sedative dulled his senses. "Damn you, Angelo." He gripped Maggie's hand as his hold on the surroundings faded. "Take care…of her…"

CHAPTER EIGHTEEN

"HE'LL BE OUT FOR A WHILE," Angelo said after he and his bodyguard, Stamos, had carried Nick into Angelo's house on the small, quiet Greek island of Patmos and laid his lifeless form on the bed in the largest of the bedrooms.

Maggie was too preoccupied to pay much attention to the surroundings. What she did notice was basic. Beautiful seaside home with whitewashed walls and blue shutters. The sound of waves in the background, a warm ocean breeze blowing in off the water. But first things first. She glanced at her cell phone display. Still no coverage. "Do you have a phone here?" she asked Angelo. "So I can call my sisters?"

"Not at the house, I'm afraid. In Skala, the main town, you'll find one."

"Thank you, Angelo. For everything."

He smiled and patted her shoulder. "You might as well get some rest, Maggie."

She nodded, too exhausted to argue. Nick was still wearing his shoes. How could a man rest properly with shoes on his feet?

Uncaring as to what was going on behind her in the main area of the cottage, Maggie focused on Nick. It felt good to finally be doing something productive. She slipped off his shoes and socks, his pants. After opening the window to freshen the air in the stuffy room, she moved his limbs and torso into a comfortable position and rearranged the pillow under his head. He didn't awaken for any of it.

After washing his face and hands with a hot cloth, she lightly touched the scars on his cheek and chest. They'd no doubt come from the car bombing that had killed Yanni. She could only imagine how deep those cuts had been, how many stitches it'd taken to patch him back up. But his worst scars, the pain of losing someone he loved went so much deeper than these.

Maggie tried to put herself in his shoes. To what lengths would she go if someone had murdered her mother, hurt Kate or Shannon? Given what she'd done to pay her mother's medical bills, Maggie could hardly blame Nick for using her and her company to gain information. He'd harmed no one. Yet.

She covered him with a light quilt and then went to shutter the window. Bright, clear sunshine streamed into the room. The sky over the Aegean Sea was the largest span of uninterrupted blue Maggie had ever seen. Not a cloud was visible on the horizon in any direction. The afternoon sun beat down, hot and unrelenting, probably a day not unlike what the residents of Patmos dealt with any of the other three hundred and sixty-four days of the year. For Maggie, though, this day was like no other day in her life.

She sat down on the edge of the bed. She couldn't have said for how long. As best she could, she processed the events. She'd been kidnapped, tied up and shot at, and now she was hiding away from an assassin. Nick was lying in front of her with a gunshot wound, having lost so much blood he looked almost as pale as the villa's plaster walls.

None of it seemed real. Maggie hadn't felt this helpless since her mother had lay dying in that hospital bed. How had she lost control?

Control? What control? She laughed to herself.

She sure as hell didn't have it now, never had, no matter how much in the past she'd deluded herself into thinking she did. All those years of busting her butt making sure she and her sisters could stand on their own two feet, and, in the end, she'd accomplished nothing, only come full circle. The harder and faster she worked to pull everything together, the more everything spun away from her. Maggie's life was out of her hands.

DIMLY, NICK BECAME AWARE of a feather pillow beneath his head and the scent of sheets dried in fresh sea air, like the linens at his grandmother's house on Crete. He took a slow, shallow breath and swore he could smell a hint of freshly baked sesame seed bread underlying the spicy aroma of homemade sausage. There was lemon and mint and garlic all combined with the warm ocean breeze blowing through an open window. The smells of Greece. Comfort. Nostalgia.

Then panic hit him in a wave. Where the hell was Maggie? He moved and a sharp pain in his side shot down the length of him. *Oh, yeah, a bullet, that's right.*

Foggy memories filtered back to him. He saw Maggie's still body lying in the dust, the image of Tarik touching her, then her face, close to him with the pungent smells of a marina filling his senses. He'd been shot, drugged, then hauled across the Aegean on a smuggler's boat. Damn that Angelo! Where did he say he was taking them?

Still groggy, with a mouth that felt stuffed with

cotton, Nick glanced around. The room held the double
bed he was lying on as well as a scarred, well-used
cedar dresser. Maggie's suitcase was sitting open next
to a new black duffle bag stacked with clothing she'd
probably purchased for him. The wood floor was
covered with a brightly colored, handmade throw rug,
similar to the ones he'd watched his grandmother
weave. Lacy, white cotton curtains fluttered in the partially opened window, and a bright sun was near to
setting behind a craggy coastline. He knew this house.
Angelo's family home on Patmos.

Nick pushed himself into a sitting position. Nausea
rolled through him. He took a deep breath and waited.
As his stomach settled, the sound of hushed voices
filtered in through the closed door. There was at least
one other person with Maggie. Her voice was soothing,
almost musical, sifting through him like a cool evening
breeze after a dreadfully hot day on the beach. She was
laughing now, softly.

He closed his eyes, letting the sound wash through
him and wishing that Tarik and Stephano had been
dealt with and he and Maggie were on holiday. The
reality was he could spend a day, maybe two, recovering on Patmos then he'd have to get back to Athens.
Maggie needed to be on her way back to D.C. as
quickly as possible.

Gingerly, he stepped into a pair of shorts and slipped
a shirt onto one arm, not bothering to button it up the front.
Slowly, he made his way to the door and eased it open.

Maggie was at the table playing cards with a man
Nick wasn't sure he recognized. He nodded at the
hulking man at the table. "Who are you?"

"Stamos," he said, standing.

"Angelo's bodyguard." Maggie crossed the room. "How are you feeling?"

Stamos quietly left the house.

"Dizzy." He closed his eyes and leaned against the doorjamb. The smell of lamb and some kind of simmering soup or stew made his empty stomach grumble loudly. "How long have I been out?"

She slipped the shirt onto his other arm and buttoned the front. "You've been sleeping almost twenty-four hours."

"Sleeping? Like hell! Where's Angelo?"

"After settling us in yesterday, he went back to Athens."

Nick barely heard what she'd said. He'd opened his eyes to look at her, and all he could focus on was the dark purple bruise marring her forehead and right side of her face. Her one eye was bloodshot and swollen. "Oh, Maggie," he whispered, "What have I done to you?"

After finishing with the last button, she glanced up at him. Her eyes were filled with so many emotions, he couldn't begin to name them. "It looks worse than it feels."

"You're going back to D.C. tonight."

"I'm not going anywhere until you're better."

He glared at her, she glared back and a tension-filled silence filled the warm air. Finally, she pulled out a chair. "Sit down before you fall down."

She was right. He was too weak to do much of anything. He nearly collapsed at the table, and she brought him a bowl of broad bean stew and a chunk of thick, crusty bread. After the first savory spoonful, Nick realized how hungry he was. After two more bowls, he felt his energy coming back.

"Any word from Kate?" he asked.

"I checked in with her yesterday when I went into town for supplies."

"And?"

"No one followed them home. They're safe. Riley is practically stitched to Kate's side, driving her crazy."

"Good." Nick smiled weakly. He grabbed her hand and pulled her down into the chair next to him. "I'm sorry if this has messed with your systems project."

"I called Alex, too. Gave him some instructions, set him on track and offered him a bonus for handling this. The A-Team will be okay for a few days, and Shannon's available by phone. She's got everything at the office under control." She grinned. "Heck, this is almost a vacation."

"Go home, Maggie." He reached over, carefully touched the swelling by her eyes. "This isn't your fight."

"It's not yours, either."

FOR THE NEXT TWO DAYS Nick rested while Maggie checked out a few of the tourist spots on the island, including the Monastery of St. John, where the disciple was said to have written the Book of Revelations in a mountainside cave. She came back to the villa replete with pictures and running at the mouth in awe and excitement. Both Maggie and Nick did their fair share of relaxing and ate an abundance of wonderful food.

In Skala, Patmos's main town, an arching strip of land that provided shelter for the myriad yachts docked in the bay, the *tavernas* offered the tastiest grilled fish platters, the *patisseries* cooked eggplant pancakes similar to those Nick had enjoyed as a child and the markets sold, among an array of other fresh items, *chorizo* and *manchego*, Spanish sausage and cheese.

They ended the third day with a dinner of *Barbounia*,

a red mullet fish, stuffed peppers and eggplant. Church bells sounded softly through the small town. "Are you feeling up to a walk?" Maggie asked. "I read there's a beach not far from here."

"Meloi," he said. "There are probably close to twenty beaches on this small island. The famous beach of multicolored stones is Lambi. Want a nude beach?" he said, grinning, "Psili Ammos."

"I'll stick with the sand and a sunset, please."

"Ah, that settles it then. Holhaka. It's a bit longer of a walk than Meloi, but it faces west." Nick bought a bottle of wine and two glasses on his way out of the restaurant and led the way down the street. Stamos followed at a discreet distance, ever watchful.

"Isn't this the island you spent quite a bit of time on as a child?" Maggie asked, grabbing his hand.

"Yeah." He squeezed her fingers. For a few moments here and there, Nick caught himself forgetting why they were on Patmos and fooling himself into believing they were on a vacation of sorts. Then the bullet wound in his side would throb and he'd be forced to remember.

Every minute he found himself torn between wanting to get close to Maggie, making the most out of his dwindling time with her, and keeping his distance, enabling him to stay focused on avenging Yanni's murder and protecting Maggie. From him.

While they followed the road out of town, she peppered him with questions about his time on Patmos.

"Yanni only came along once on a trip here," he explained. "So I spent most of my time alone. Entertaining myself. Swimming. Snorkeling. Fishing."

"You never met any of the other kids?"

"You sound like my mother did back then. Why

bother? I was content alone." They reached a path familiar to Nick, a shortcut to Holhaka through the brush. "This way." He grabbed her hand and pulled her behind him.

They pushed through the bush and came onto the beach, a wide expanse of pebbly sand. A slight breeze blew in off the bay, and clouds scattered across the darkening sky. They sat beneath a tamarisk and looked out at the calm waters of the Aegean as the sun dipped low in the sky.

The water, brilliant hues of blue and purple, turned bloodred where it caught the sun's fading rays. A white fishing boat chugged slowly across the bay, making small waves, ripples through the water colors.

Maggie sighed and shifted closer to Nick, rested her cheek on his chest. He touched his lips to the top of her head and marveled at the softness of her curls.

"Are the sunsets always the same?"

"No. Sometimes they're full of pastels. Rose, lavender, gray. Sometimes the sky's all red, except for the deep orange of the sun. I've seen bright fuchsias and purples you wouldn't believe could possibly be real if you saw them in a painting. It's different every night."

He closed his eyes, not really caring about the sunset. He wanted only to commit to memory the feeling of the weight of her on his chest, near his heart.

"We could stay here forever," she whispered. "Forget the rest of the world."

He said nothing, for there was nothing he *could* say to make her understand. He and Maggie could have no life together until this was settled, then he'd be whole again, complete, ready to share the future with her.

Tomorrow, he'd have to send her away.

CHAPTER NINETEEN

MAGGIE AWOKE in the middle of the night. She'd insisted on sleeping in the room with Nick, claiming it would be convenient. She'd be able to get anything he needed, so he wouldn't have to get out of bed. In truth, it was only an excuse to be near him.

Right now, though, something seemed wrong, as if the still air was charged with energy. Bright moonlight streamed through the window, illuminating the room as if it were early morning. She turned her head. Nick was wide awake, on his side, staring at her.

"You sound like a kitten when you snore," he whispered.

"I do not snore."

His answering smile, sad and introspective, never made it to his eyes.

"Are you all right?" she asked.

"I'm fine."

"Do you need anything?"

His eyelids seemed to grow heavy as if he were enduring great pain. "Only you."

For a moment, Maggie couldn't move. Had she heard him right? Was she dreaming? She stared into his eyes, looking for an answer. Then slowly, slowly, giving him every chance in the world to back away, she leaned forward and pressed her lips against his.

The kiss started slow and unhurried, as if they had all the time in the world, as if a coldhearted killer wasn't after them. Both warm with sleep, their bodies were relaxed and peaceful. His mouth pressed softly against hers, his tongue danced a measured waltz, his hand lazied its way over her arm.

"Mmm." Maggie inched her hand under his T-shirt, up the flat, hard plane of his stomach. The ripple of old scar tissue on his chest took on new meaning. The bullet wound on his side would heal, but now he'd have a new scar, a larger one. All because of Yanni. If Nick could love her half as much as he'd loved Yanni, maybe she could convince him to drop this madness and come home with her.

She spread her hands on his chest, kneaded his muscles, and felt his heart racing beneath her hand. She sat up. This time, nothing, no one was going to stop her. Not wanting to hurt him by pulling his shirt over his head, she bit through the hem at the bottom and tore it off him. His boxers were gone in a second. He was naked. And he was all hers.

She whipped off her own boxers and T-shirt, and his eyes caught fire. "Maggie, slow down."

"No. I've had enough of slow and soft." She could feel herself, swollen, wet and aching to have him. Straddling him, she eased him inside her and kissed him, deeply. His breathing turned ragged as she moved over him. Slowly at first, like the kiss that had started all this. Then her center spiraled with wonderful tension. Faster and faster, she let herself go.

When Nick cupped her breasts, the sensations at her nipples moved straight through her.

"Now, Maggie," he whispered. "This is yours."

She couldn't breathe, couldn't think. This—this—was what sex with love was all about. All she knew was the pressure of him against her, inside her.

"Let go, Maggie."

So close. Closer and closer. Finally, she felt herself flying. "Nick!" she cried, mindless, grabbing him and holding on. "I can't believe it," she whispered.

Nick shuddered. He buried his face in her neck, pressed his mouth against her skin and groaned. Another thrust against her, and she orgasmed again. Again. This time, taking him with her.

When she finally stopped, she laughed, tightened her hold on him and kissed him. "That was better than I'd ever imagined it could be."

Nick closed his eyes, letting the lingering feel of her fingertips on his lips, his neck, his shoulders wash over him. Oh, what heaven to know this woman's not-so-soft insistence, to be wanted by Maggie. The warmth of her hands, resting on his chest, spread through him and gathered in another rock-hard erection. Apparently, he wasn't finished with her.

"Now I get it." She grinned, contentment spreading across her gorgeous face.

"You get fast," he murmured against her collarbone. Carefully, he rolled her off him and kissed his way down the butterfly tattoos along her side. When he got to her hip, he pushed her onto her back and spread her legs. He glanced at her and whispered, "Now are you ready for slow?"

SMOKE. FLAMES. *No. No!* Nick jolted awake, his heart racing and his chest on fire. The dream. Again.

By now, he was used to the varied beginnings. Sometimes he and Yanni were walking along the beaches of the Aegean Sea. Other times they were goofing off in school. But the nightmare always ended the same. Yanni's face, contorted in pain, the sound of his voice pleading for Nick to *do* something. Kyrena's scream. Then the same intense explosion that left him blinded and impossibly weak for the first few moments after waking.

He closed his eyes.

Only this time it hadn't been Yanni who'd blown up in front of Nick. And the screams? They weren't Kyrena's. This time the face in the car had been Maggie's. It was the sound of her pain that had filled him with dread.

Nick carefully folded back the covers. Though it was only four o'clock in the morning, he knew from experience he would be unable to sleep for the rest of the night. There was no point in fighting it. Quietly, hoping to not disturb Maggie, Nick grabbed a pair of pants and a shirt and left the room.

He dressed and was finishing packing all of Maggie's belongings when Stamos awoke. "As soon as Maggie wakes up, take her back to Athens and get her home to D.C."

Stamos nodded, and Nick set her suitcases near the door before going outside. Leaning against the gnarly trunk of a tamarisk, he sat at the cliff's edge and waited for dawn.

He should never have made love to her. Her touch, her laugh, the feeling of being inside her only confused him all the more. Before Maggie had come into his life, Nick had known who he was, what he was doing and why. His life had purpose, focus and meaning. He'd understood his place in the world. Maggie had changed everything, blurring every one of his lines. Now, he saw clear distinction in nothing.

Why? Why Maggie? Even before Yanni's death Nick had found women inconsequential. Other than his mother and Kyrena, not a single woman had touched his heart in any way other than friendship, but how could a man possibly go about trivializing someone like Maggie? With her unabashed manners, her in-your-face presence, how could Nick not be captivated?

She was red to his black, sound to his silence. When he pushed, she pushed back. Maggie was the woman he'd been looking for his entire life, and he hadn't known until this moment he'd been searching. He respected her, trusted her. Loved her. He loved her and it changed absolutely nothing. Knowing what he'd be losing only made what he had to do all the more difficult.

As the first of the sun's rays blazed across the water, he felt her presence, changing the direction of the wind, altering his world. Maggie knelt behind him, leaned her cheek on his shoulder. "Morning."

He could hear the smile, the contentment, in her voice. "Morning."

"You're cold." She wrapped her arms around him.

He closed his eyes, wanted to delay the inevitable, knowing there was no point. "Maggie...I...need to be away from you."

"That explains my bag by the door." She pulled away and a chill hit his back. "Why?"

"You're too distracting. I need to refocus. I'm so close to righting a wrong."

"Murder sounds so harmless when you put it that way."

"That's how you think of me?" He turned. "As a murderer?"

"No." She studied his face, shook her head. "I know the kind of tenderness and compassion you're capable of, but if you follow through with your plan, you will be a murderer."

"If I don't, I'll be only half a man." He cocked his head toward her. "You can't understand, can you?"

"Not when you can tell everything you know to Giannis and let the Greek authorities do their job."

"Maggie, Giannis could be protecting whoever hired Tarik."

"Then go to someone else."

"They've had five years to deal with this."

"Identify Tarik. Give them the picture, maybe then they'd have a chance."

His eyes narrowed.

"Back in D.C., I logged onto your laptop," she offered at his silent question, "trying to find out what you were doing. I found Angelo's e-mail."

"After what I did, I can't blame you, can I?"

"Angelo thinks you should turn the photo over to Giannis."

"Well, Angelo doesn't know what he's talking about. Identifying Tarik wouldn't solve a damn thing. They'd have a face to go with a name, and faces can easily be changed."

"You could give the Greek authorities a chance, couldn't you? A few months, a few weeks? Anything. If they did find him, you'd *be* avenged."

"This isn't about me. This is about Yanni."

"This is totally about you, Nick. Yanni is dead. You're not. Listen to what you know to be right in your heart. For us. For what we could have together."

His heart? Maybe that was why it hurt so much to look at her and know she would be leaving in a few hours. At that moment he wished he were another man.

He wished his obligation to avenge Yanni's death could be fulfilled by someone else. Someone stronger. Someone who wouldn't be tempted to set aside his convictions for a woman.

It only proved how weak he was. He wanted a life. He wanted Maggie. If he gave in, what kind of man would he be? Who would he become? His life would turn sour and he'd sour everyone around him. "Without honor, I'm nothing. I can give you nothing."

"I can't accept that." She shook her head. "Despite not being entirely honest with me at first, you are the most honorable man I have ever met. There is no one I know who would sacrifice five years of his life to protect a woman and her children. To treat her as a sister when he could've taken advantage of the situation. To build a business and sell it so that she wouldn't ever have to worry about finances. That's true honor, Nick. Not this eye-for-an-eye crap."

"Honor means different things for different people. I know what I have to do. We can have nothing together until Stephano and Tarik are dead."

"And if it's by your hands, you'll have destroyed our future as well."

She was right. Another certainty died.

He'd believed peace would come to him after he'd avenged Yanni, then he and Maggie could pick up where they'd left off. Only Maggie wasn't the shrewd businesswoman who cared for nothing and no one, nor the irreverent, unprincipled hacker. She was the tender-hearted soul who'd given her life for her sisters. She was also opinionated, passionate, and as black and white in her convictions as him.

Nick wouldn't be able live with himself until he saw

this thing through. Maggie wouldn't be able to live with Nick if he did. It was over. He refused to drag her down with him. He not only had to let her go, he had to make her go.

"Yanni was my friend." Nick turned back toward the ocean and faced the sun. "I owe this to him."

"And what am I?" she asked. "What do you owe me?"

"Nothing." Pushing her away was going to almost kill him. "I owe you nothing."

"How can you say that?" she cried. "I love you! The way you've touched me, made love with me only a few hours ago. I know you love me, too."

"I thought you understood." He shook his head.

"No. You're pushing me away. Again."

"I made it very clear, Maggie. No future. No tomorrows. I never promised anything."

"You don't have to say anything to promise *everything*. I felt it in your hands stronger than any words could've ever been. I saw it in your eyes." She caressed his cheek and turned his head, forcing him to look at her. "Every time you touch me, every time you look at me, you promise to love me. Forever."

She was right, and he would. Love her forever.

"Don't throw that away," she whispered.

He turned, unable to look at her. "Go back to D.C., Maggie. Forget about me."

She knelt in front of him and kissed him, softly, making no demands, saying goodbye. He closed his eyes, refused to kiss her back.

"Angelo told me another proverb on the boat ride over here," she whispered against his mouth. "If someone among you sees wrong, he must right it by his hand if he can. If he cannot, then by his tongue. If he cannot, then by his gaze. And if he cannot, then in his heart. You have the power in your heart to let this go, Nick."

"Goodbye, Maggie." He took her arms and set her away from him. "Be careful."

"So that's it then? There's nothing I can say, nothing I can do?" Maggie stood. "I wish you'd never come into my life."

That hurt, more than any bullet ever could. When he heard the sound of the car doors opening and closing, he couldn't risk turning around for one last look. The car drove away, and Nick remained on the sandy beach, savoring the lingering feel of Maggie's mouth against his. Then, on his lips, he tasted the pure, salty remnants of her tears mingling with his own.

Tarik. Stephano. Now they could both come. Nick would finish this, one way or another.

CHAPTER TWENTY

"LET GO OF ME!" Shannon yanked her arm from the blond giant's grasp and barged into the greenhouse. "Maggie, what the hell is going on? And who is this...ape?"

Maggie fussed with the new array of plants she'd bought that morning, but even the relative peace and quiet of her greenhouse hadn't cleared away the black mood that had swept over her the moment she'd arrived back home late last night.

The gray day outside wasn't helping matters. A heavy downpour of rain might have been relief of sorts. Instead, all day, light, unrelenting droplets of moisture had fallen steadily from an unending ceiling of clouds. The air seemed oppressive in thickness.

"Maggie, are you listening to me?" Shannon took a few tentative steps into the humid room. "Tell this Neanderthal to get lost."

"Stamos, the greenhouse is off limits." Maggie's voice sounded hollow even to herself. "There's no way in here, anyway, except through the apartment. Unless you're Spiderman and come in off the roof."

"Maggie—"

"Please." She heard the big man's frustrated sigh, then the soft click of the latch. Without looking, she knew he'd be stationed on the other side of the doors.

"So what's with him and the guy Kate brought with her?" Shannon's high heels tapped across the hard flagstone. "Kate sure as hell didn't say much."

"Bodyguards. Nick sent them back with us."

"Wasn't Nick sufficiently guarding your body?"

Maggie turned around and glared at her sister. "Sometimes, Shannon, you're about as sensitive as a pit bull."

Shannon sucked in a quick breath. "What happened to your face?" She led Maggie over to the chaise and sat down next to her.

Half an hour later, Maggie finished her explanation of all that had transpired since she and Kate had left D.C. "So that's it. Everything in a nutshell."

Shannon sat still. "Are you okay?"

"It's only bruising. I'll be—"

"That's not what I'm talking about."

Maggie eased herself slowly from the chair and wandered back over to her potting table, afraid if she talked about Nick, she wouldn't be able to staunch the flow of tears.

"Well, that settles it." Shannon stood. "With everything you're going through, there's no way Craig is talking me into that Caribbean cruise."

"Was this supposed to be a honeymoon?" Maggie turned in surprise.

"Hardly," Shannon said. "He and that Barbie doll from General Walker's party were planning on going, and Craig convinced me it would be a shame to waste the tickets."

"It would be. You and Craig could use the time alone before facing his family."

"We're supposed to head out this afternoon. I'm not going to leave you alone. Or Kate."

"Riley can take care of Kate," Maggie said. Besides which, Kate was quite happily ensconced practically twenty-four-seven in Rufus's studio. "We don't need you at the office. The A-Team's doing great on the new project," she said, faking as bright a smile as she could muster. "Go. We'll be fine."

"I'm not going," Shannon said, putting her hands on her hips. "I am, though, taking the afternoon off to break it to Craig. You don't get to decide this, do you?"

Maggie took a deep breath. "No, I don't."

"Well." Shannon smiled. "I'm glad that's finally settled."

"YOU'RE PLANNING ON GOING BACK to Athens today?" Angelo said, shaking his head.

"My side is nearly healed." Nick did his best to ignore his old friend and continued staring at the glowing orange ball of the early morning sunrise. The previous night had been miserable enough without this unfortunate interruption. "I'll be on the next ferry out this morning."

"And how long have you been out here, staring at the water?"

Since Maggie had left early yesterday. He'd returned to the cottage once for some food, but he'd been drawn too many times to the bedroom he'd shared with Maggie. After finding she'd left the Heart of Artemis necklace for him on top of the dresser, he could no longer stand that cottage. She was amazing, turning it into a key. And no matter how hard he worked at it, he couldn't figure out how to turn it back into a box.

Angelo snorted. "So what do you think is going to come rolling in off the waves? Berk Tarik, Stephano?"

"Go away, Angelo." Nick turned on him, venting an

entire day's worth of pent-up anger and frustration. "You're a meddling old man. If I wasn't so preoccupied at the moment, I'd give you more than a piece of my mind for your interference in this whole mess."

"So you think I should have let you stay in Athens injured and weak?"

"Sending Maggie here to Patmos with me was a bad idea."

"Ah, I see," Angelo murmured. "Where is she?"

"I sent her home."

"Back to D.C.?"

"Yesterday morning."

"When a fox cannot reach the grapes, he says they are not ripe," Angelo murmured.

Nick groaned.

Angelo started pacing. "Did you at least send Stamos back with her?"

"Yes!" Nick stood at the sound of apprehension in the old man's voice. "Dammit, Angelo, what is it?"

"After getting you and Maggie here, I gave Giannis Ramos Tarik's picture. Late last night, Giannis's people found and arrested him."

"Finally." Nick tried to summon any amount of regret that he hadn't been the one to take Tarik down, but, surprisingly, all he felt was relief. "Is he talking?"

"My sources confirmed he gave them names, dates, everything they want."

"Who hired him?"

"You were right all along. Stephano. Giannis had his suspicions, but they could prove nothing."

"I'd like to see that sonofabitch get out of this one."

"He already has."

"What?" Nick turned, on alert.

"Stephano left Athens very early this morning. He boarded a flight to Washington, D.C."

"How 'BOUT YOU make yourself at home on the couch in my office tonight," Maggie said to Stamos as they stepped off the elevator. She hadn't really wanted a walk in the park or been hungry for Chinese, but she'd sorely needed the break from her office and the exercise.

"Not a good idea," he said from only two steps behind her. "I'm staying in your apartment. Like last night."

She unlocked her office door and ignored the blinking light on her phone indicating several messages had been left while she and Stamos had been gone. She'd have the rest of her life to work.

"There's a pizza joint a few blocks down if you get hungry later on." Maggie climbed the stairs to her apartment.

"If I get hungry," Stamos said, "I'll call out for something."

Maggie stopped abruptly on the steps and turned around. Stamos, so close on her heels, nearly bumped into her. It was late, Maggie was emotionally wrung out, and this annoyingly thorough bodyguard had been sticking to her like glue for more than forty-eight hours. Her apartment was her only chance at a sanctuary.

"Look. You were here all day and no one the least bit threatening ever came around. We locked up everything before we left earlier, so no one could have gotten in to the office while we were gone, let alone my apartment. Let's call it a night right here, so I can have some time alone. Okay?"

"I'm not supposed to leave you alone for a minute. Nick said—"

"I don't care what Nick said! He's not here now. He'll never be here again. To hell with Nick Ballos!" She ran up the remaining steps, slammed her apartment door in Stamos's face and locked it, the bolt making a clean, satisfying click as it slid in place. She'd no sooner turned around than her apartment phone started ringing.

Sighing heavily, she switched it off, letting the answering service take it. She could hear Stamos going back down the steps. She was alone. Finally. Turning around, she stared out the window. From here she could see the spot where Kyrena's limo had pulled into the parking lot next to Nick. Had that really only been a little more than two weeks ago?

Maggie would give anything to go back in time, to that day Shannon had walked into her office with a file on the perfect man for Maggie. Mr. Right. If only she could go back in time and listen more closely to her own intuition. Nick Ballos was lethal, all right, to her heart.

She thought of the last words she'd said to him, wishing he'd never come into her life. It wasn't true. She couldn't honestly regret a moment of her time with him. She only wished there'd been more. She closed her eyes, her shoulders sagging in resignation. "Nick," she whispered into the still darkness, "come back to me."

"Oh, I think he will." A man's deep, heavily accented voice sounded quietly near Maggie's ear. Then a warm hand swiftly clamped over her mouth and something hard jabbed into the base of her skull. "Make one sound, and you'll never see Nick Ballos again. Cooperate, yes?"

The voice was faintly familiar, but chilling. Without moving her head, she scanned her apartment for anything she might use as a weapon. Nothing was within easy reach. She had no other option except to nod.

Slowly, the man moved his hand away, leaving a salty residue on her lips. She wiped her mouth, then turned around. A profile became discernable in the faint glow of city lights through the window. "Stephano."

"Silence." Keeping the gun pointed directly at Maggie, he reached over and quietly unlocked the bolt on the door. "When Nick gets here, we want him to be able to get in, don't we?"

"What makes you think he'll come?"

"He'll come."

After her last conversation with him on Patmos, Maggie wasn't so sure. "How did you get into my apartment?" she whispered.

"Climbed onto your roof from the neighboring building. You really should lock all your doors." He motioned behind him. "Now move. Out onto the roof."

Maggie threw open the heavy French doors off her bedroom and stepped into the moist warm air of her greenhouse. "What do you want out here?"

"Turn on the lights." He jabbed her with the gun.

She flipped the switch near the side of the door and fear raced through her at the sight of Stephano. He looked nothing like the calm, poised man she'd met at Giannis's home. This man looked wild, possessed, his hair disheveled, his eyes bloodshot and shifting frantically.

"Put your hands behind your back." He had two sets of handcuffs and slapped one on Maggie. "Now. Outside. Onto the roof."

"Why?"

"Onto…the roof." He pushed her outside, slamming the door shut behind them. Though the rain had stopped a short time ago, the warm evening air blowing across her sweat-dampened skin was still humid and thick.

Stephano paced back and forth, and Maggie's fear escalated with every slap of his shoes in the shallow puddles on the surface of the tarred roof. This was driving her crazy. "So now what?" she asked.

"We wait."

"For what?"

"The end." A smile spread across his face as he viewed the fully lit greenhouse with apparent satisfaction. "When Nick walks into the greenhouse through your bedroom door, he'll be a sitting duck."

Stephano was right. The inside of the greenhouse was a beacon in the black night sky. If Nick did come after her, he'd need a miracle to make it out to the roof. Or at least a diversion.

"Lie down," Stephano said. "On your stomach. Now."

She found a position where she could still see the French doors leading into her bedroom. Blood pounded in her ears, her breathing grew shallow. *Think. Think.* Five seconds. That's all. Five seconds to distract Stephano and give Nick the opportunity to get into the greenhouse and shut off the lights. Without that five second window, he didn't have a chance.

Maggie forced herself to take deep, slow breaths and unflinchingly kept her gaze on those doors. She had no clue how much time passed, but if Nick did come, whether it was in three hours or three minutes, she had to be ready. Somehow, she had to be ready.

Then there it was! She saw a hand on the floor creeping from her bedroom into the greenhouse. Someone was on the floor crawling toward them.

CHAPTER TWENTY-ONE

MAGGIE PRAYED the first words she uttered would sound level and calm. "Nick and I had a big fight, Stephano," she said, taking a breath to keep the words from tumbling out of her mouth. "You're crazy for thinking he'll come back to D.C. for me."

Stephano laughed and glanced back at Maggie. Past Stephano, Maggie saw Nick poke his head through the door and assess the greenhouse. He was here. He did come. Quickly, he slid on his belly across the flagstone toward the door to the roof.

My God, what was he doing? He should shut off the light.

"He'll come," Stephano said softly. "He gave you the Heart of Artemis, didn't he?"

"I gave the necklace back to him," Maggie interrupted as Stephano was about to turn back to face the entrance to the roof. "I think that sent a pretty strong message."

"Returning the necklace doesn't change the fact that he gave it to you in the first place. He knows what that pendant means. You are his life."

"You're wrong. He's probably in Athens right now, looking for you," Maggie continued quickly. Nick was halfway to the door. Halfway. "He doesn't care about me. All he cares about is avenging Yanni's death."

"So whether he comes for you or for me—" Stephano shrugged his shoulders "—he'll still come."

"I think you're wrong—"

Stephano turned. Maggie held her breath.

The greenhouse lights went out, and the roof plunged into darkness. Stephano fired off several shots. Amidst the echoing sound of gunfire and shattering glass, he grabbed Maggie and dragged her backward.

"Make one more move, Nick," Stephano yelled, "and Maggie dies. It's very simple." He held the gun to Maggie's temple.

Darkness and a painful silence filled the night air. One of the gunshots, wild though they were, could have hit Nick. The image of him bleeding and dying on her greenhouse floor clawed at Maggie. "Nick!" she screamed and struggled to break Stephano's grip. The gun knocked against Maggie's forehead.

"I will kill you," he whispered.

"Let her go, Stephano." Nick's voice sounded deep and calm. He hadn't been shot. "This is between you and me."

Slowly, Maggie's eyes adjusted to the darkness. Every pane of glass this side of the greenhouse had completely shattered from the bullets. The rest of it seemed unaffected, except for an overturned bench near the door to the roof. Stephano seemed to focus on it an instant before Maggie.

"Throw out your weapon," he demanded. "Then I'll let her go."

"No, Nick!" Maggie cried. "Don't—"

Nick felt as much as heard the smack as Stephano's gun connected with Maggie's head. He quickly slid his gun across the wet surface of the roof. "There! I'm unarmed. Let her go."

Stephano loosened his grip, and, slightly dazed by the blow to her head, Maggie fell limp to the rooftop. Stephano pointed the gun at Nick. "Move away from the bench."

Nick stepped into full view. "It's over, Stephano. Stamos is calling the police right now. They'll be here any minute."

"So this hasn't worked out exactly as I planned." Stephano's lips twisted into a smile. "No matter, an end is an end. I believe she'll go first." He pointed the gun at Maggie. "How does it feel, Nick?" Stephano glared at him. "To have something you desperately want taken away from you?"

"Kyrena was never yours to begin with."

"She would've been! If you hadn't gotten in the way." Stephano's hand trembled with anger. "Now I'm getting…in *your* way."

"Leave her out of this. She's not responsible for anything you or I have done." Slowly, Nick moved closer. "I'll make a deal with you. Tell me where to find Kyrena. And Maggie's free to go."

Maggie's head moved, almost imperceptibly, from side to side, silently urging him not to say anything. His expression softened slightly before he turned back to Stephano.

"So you still want to find Kyrena?"

Stephano moved the gun closer to Maggie's head.

"Doesn't it just kill you that Yanni had her first?" Nick said, his voice taunting. "Then just when you were ready to make her yours, *I* took her away. I made her my *wife*."

"You're playing with fire, Ballos."

Nick grinned. "Things were good between Kyrena and me. Very…good."

"So you want to go first!" Stephano swung back at Nick. His face turned blotchy with hatred.

Maggie shivered as Stephano took aim at Nick. She drew back her legs and kicked him.

Stephano's knees buckled. Nick lunged forward as a shot went wild into the sky. He knocked the gun from Stephano's hand. They struggled, backing toward the roof's concrete half wall. Maggie wriggled toward the gun. Stephano threw a kick that landed solid in Nick's gut. Nick doubled over and landed stomach down on the rooftop.

Stephano dropped on top of him, grabbed Nick's hand and slapped one cuff on Nick's wrist and the other on his own, binding them together. But as he pulled the cuffs out of his pocket, Maggie heard the keys drop onto the rooftop.

"Where I go, you go!" Stephano yelled. He lunged for Nick, pushing them both closer to the edge of the roof. When he slipped on the slick rooftop, Stephano flew over Nick's bent form and flipped partway over the half wall. He teetered on the edge, his legs dangling over the side of the building.

Behind him, Maggie screamed, "Drop him! Let him go!" She grabbed the gun, rolled to the keys, and worked to get the handcuffs off her wrists.

"I can't! We're cuffed together." Nick's feet slipped on the wet roof. Stephano was pulling, dragging Nick closer and closer to the wall. "What the hell are you doing?" Nick yelled. "You're going to pull us both over."

A calm, determined, almost peaceful look overtook Stephano's features. "I have nothing to live for, Nick. I'm better off dead."

Strange, Nick thought, for five years he'd been readying himself for this moment, preparing himself for the possibility of death. Now, all he had to do was let go, and it would be over. Vengeance would at long last be served.

"Nick!" Maggie cried. He could hear her shuffling toward him across the surface of the roof.

"Come with me, Nick," Stephano urged him. "Let's finish this. It's what you've been wanting. For five long years!"

Yes, he'd been ready to die. Before Maggie. If Nick let go, Stephano would win. Again. The metal cuff dug painfully into his wrist, making it feel as if Stephano's weight might actually yank off his hand.

"Don't do it!" Maggie pleaded. "Please! Think about one thing. Please. Did you come here to kill Stephano? Or to help me?"

She was right. He could feel it in his heart.

The moment Angelo had told him that Stephano had come to D.C., his first thought had been for Maggie, not Stephano. Maggie had changed everything, even him. Stephano's life might be over, but Nick's wasn't. He had so much to look forward to, so much to live for. With Maggie. The only way she'd come to him was to end this now.

"Enough!" he yelled. Gripping his hands around Stephano's wrist, Nick slowly, steadily pulled Stephano toward him.

"No!" Stephano resisted, pulling back. "We're going down!"

"Not tonight," Maggie yelled.

Nick felt Maggie's free arms go around his waist, stabilizing him. It was all the leverage he needed. Slowly, inch by straining inch, they hauled Stephano off the edge of the wall and back onto the roof.

"No! No! No!" Stephano yelled.

"Nick, take the gun!"

He grabbed the gun and Maggie quickly unlocked the handcuffs. Then Nick jumped back, shielding Maggie behind him. "It's over." He pointed the gun at Stephano. "You're going back to Greece and answering for Yanni's murder."

Stephano backed away from them, bent over and panting like a enraged wild animal. "No!" He lunged forward and dove at Nick, trying once more to take them both over the edge.

"Everyone, down!" Stamos shouted from the greenhouse behind them. Gunshots pounded through the night. Stephano convulsed and flipped in midair. His body narrowly missed Nick and flew over the wall. Alone.

It was over. Nick ran to Maggie. "Are you okay?"

"I'm fine." She fell into his arms.

Within seconds, the rooftop was crammed with police. Hours later, reports had been filed, and Shannon and Kate were back at Shannon's apartment, assured all was well. Finally, blissfully alone in Maggie's kitchen, Nick turned toward Maggie and held her as tightly as he could. "I'm sorry for what I put you—"

"Shh. It's finished. Done. Over."

An incomprehensible weight lifted from Nick, unburdening him. Finally, he could breathe, live, and—he looked down at Maggie—love. "No, it's not over." He grabbed her hand and led her toward the bedroom. "This is just the beginning."

EPILOGUE

MAGGIE FINGERED the Heart of Artemis pendant while she perused the crowd inside the gallery. Young, jeans-clad college kids rubbed shoulders with high-heeled socialites, bottles of beer or fancy drinks and tasty hors d'oeuvres in hand. No one looked better or happier than Kate, and it was a good thing, too, because this was Kate's night to shine. She'd been participating with Rufus in exhibits for years, but tonight Maggie's not-so-little sister was going solo.

Kate stood toward the back of the gallery, surrounded by an adoring crowd, looking very mature for twenty-two. She'd worked incredibly hard these past years, was finally getting the critical acclaim she deserved and had found time to accumulate two years' worth of college credits. Maggie was so proud of her.

"Hey, little mama." Shannon scooted next to Maggie and patted Maggie's rounded, six-month-pregnant belly.

"Hey mama, yourself." Maggie patted back.

Their due dates were within two weeks of each other, but Shannon looked, not surprisingly, a bit bigger, given this was her second child with Craig.

"Good turnout, eh?" Shannon said.

"Sure is." There had to be over seventy people milling about. "Have you seen Mom and Dad Ballos?"

"Over there." Shannon pointed off to the left.

Never having had any daughters, Nick's mom and dad thought the sun rose and set on Maggie, Shannon and Kate. The Dillon girls, for their part, had adopted his parents as their own. Nick's parents hadn't been the only surprises tonight. Even Kyrena, Carlos, Nestor and Chrissy had come to show their support.

"I think I've heard about as many accolades about your orchids as Kate's work," Shannon said.

"Really?"

"They're beautiful, Maggie."

This was Maggie's first exhibition of sorts. After Shannon had taken over the software business, Maggie had started her own greenhouse full of exotic plants. Kate had asked her to liven up a few of the displays in the gallery for tonight, and Maggie's one-of-a-kind plants, while not as big a hit as Kate's pottery, were apparently holding their own.

Kate popped in between them, grinning from ear to ear. "So, what do you two think of all this?"

"I think," Maggie said, wrapping an arm around Kate's waist, "that Mom would be very proud of her youngest daughter. I know I am. Pretty soon we'll be seeing your work in galleries around the world."

"And I think," Shannon said, wrapping an arm around Kate's other side and forming a tight, three-sister huddle, "that if Kate were pregnant we wouldn't be able to hug like this."

They laughed.

"I got asked to do a show in L.A. next week," Kate said.

"You're off," Maggie said.

"And running," Shannon added with a grin.

"Maggie, I know you didn't think this was the best route for me," Kate said, turning serious. "Making me fight for this has made it all the more worthwhile."

"I'm glad you fought, Kate." Maggie tightened her hold around her sisters' waists. "And I'm glad you didn't, Shannon."

Shannon laughed and said, "Thanks for filling in for Mom."

"For everything you've done for us," Kate added. "We wouldn't be who we are today without you."

"Amen," Shannon added.

Maggie swallowed and shook her head. "You two are who you are regardless of me. Thanks for teaching me how to step out of the way."

"Someday," Kate said, patting Maggie's stomach, "she's going to thank me for it."

"She?" Nick's deep voice sounded behind Maggie, breaking the sisterly huddle. He wrapped an arm around her shoulder and held out a sparkling water. "Thirsty?" Nick was always attentive, but since her pregnancy, he downright pampered Maggie.

"Thank you."

"You're a hit tonight, Kate," he said.

"All the food and drinks are a hit, too." Kate kissed his cheek. "Thank you for planning all this."

"My pleasure."

Craig walked toward them with two-year-old Chad clinging to his hand. When the boy saw Nick, he broke away and ran. "Uncle Nick!"

Nick scooped him into his arms. "Hey, buddy."

Chad grabbed for his pacifier, cuddled into Nick's shoulder, and picked at the collar of Nick's dress shirt.

"He's tired, huh?"

"Yeah," Shannon said. "He was awake most of last night."

"Psych up, big guy," Craig said, mock punching Nick in the shoulder.

"Honestly?" Nick smiled down at Maggie. "I can't wait."

Maggie slid under his free arm. *I hope you're catching this, Mom, 'cause it doesn't get any better than this.* She snuggled her face into Nick's chest, almost nose to nose with Chad, massive amounts of contentment suddenly threatening to melt her bones. "Hello, sleepyhead," Maggie said to Chad.

"Hi, Mag." The tyke was having a tough time with multiple syllables.

"Sorry, guys, but we need to get Chad home," Shannon said. "Kate, honey. I'm so happy for you." Kate and Shannon hugged and everyone said goodbye to Craig, Chad and Shannon.

After they'd left, Nick stretched and said, "Maybe we should be heading home, too."

"Tired?"

"To the bone." Nick caught her gaze and smiled.

Sure you are. She grinned, knowing from prior experience exactly what he was thinking. He couldn't wait to get the hell out of here so they could make love. Maggie had to admit her thoughts were tracking along the same lines.

She must be rubbing off on him. His hair looked slightly mussed, and, heaven forbid, he hardly ever wore ties any longer. White shirts? Tonight he was actually wearing navy blue, and had left two buttons undone. She loved the way the tiniest bit of black chest hair peeked out at her. She might be six months pregnant, but that hadn't stopped her from doing anything, and she did mean anything, with Nick.

"You guys are disgusting." Kate grimaced. "Get a room."

"We will," Nick muttered. "Later."

Kate's PR person signaled her over. "Thank God, I'm being summoned." She went off to mingle.

"You doing okay?" Nick asked.

"Never better."

"Well, you've never looked better. That's for sure. Now I know what people mean by a woman glowing with pregnancy." He cupped her cheek, dug his fingers into her hair. "Your skin's like velvet. Your hair's curlier, almost as if it's happy. And your lips…" He bent his head and kissed her. "Are we really having a girl?"

"Kate was kidding." Maggie wrapped her arms around Nick's waist. "Life is good, you know?"

"Yeah, I know." He took a deep breath, rested his chin on top of her head. "That's what happens when you hook up with Mr. Right."

"Good thing I listened to you for a change." She reached up and brushed his cheek. "No regrets?"

"Never." He touched the Heart of Artemis pendant. "Yes, the key to life is love, but there's something else Yanni had figured out long before me."

"What's that?"

"He understood that there's no greater honor for a man than living and loving as a husband. A father." As he leaned into her hand and kissed her palm, he would have sworn he heard the sound of Yanni laughing. "I love you, Maggie."

"Promise?"

"In everything I do. For the rest of my life."

* * * * *

Here's a sneak peek at
THE CEO'S CHRISTMAS PROPOSITION,
the first in USA TODAY *bestselling author*
Merline Lovelace's HOLIDAYS ABROAD *trilogy*
coming in November 2008.

American Devon McShay is about to get the
Christmas surprise of a lifetime when she meets
her new client, sexy billionaire Caleb Logan, for
the very first time.

Silhouette
Desire

Available November 2008

Her breath whistled out in a sigh of relief when he exited Customs. Devon recognized him right away from the newspaper and magazine articles her friend and partner Sabrina had looked up during her frantic prep work.

Caleb John Logan, Jr. Thirty-one. Six-two. With jet-black hair, laser-blue eyes and a linebacker's shoulders under his charcoal-gray cashmere overcoat. His jaw-dropping good looks didn't score him any points with Devon. She'd learned the hard way not to trust handsome heartbreakers like Cal Logan.

But he was a client. An important one. And she was willing to give someone who'd served a hitch in the marines before earning a B.S. from the University of Oregon, an MBA from Stanford and his first million at the ripe old age of twenty-six the benefit of the doubt.

Right up until he spotted the hot-pink pashmina, that is.

Devon knew the flash of color was more visible than the sign she held up with his name on it. So she wasn't surprised when Logan picked her out of the crowd and cut in her direction. She'd just plastered on her best businesswoman smile when he whipped an arm around her waist. The next moment she was sprawled against his cashmere-covered chest.

"Hello, brown eyes."

Swooping down, he covered her mouth with his.

Sheer astonishment kept Devon rooted to the spot for a few seconds while her mind whirled chaotically. Her first thought was that her client had downed a few too many drinks during the long flight. Her second, that he'd mistaken the kind of escort and consulting services her company provided. Her third shoved everything else out of her head.

The man could kiss!

His mouth moved over hers with a skill that ignited sparks at a half dozen flash points throughout her body. Devon hadn't experienced that kind of spontaneous combustion in a while. A *long* while.

The sparks were still popping when she pushed off his chest, only now they fueled a flush of anger.

"Do you always greet women you don't know with a lip-lock, Mr. Logan?"

A smile crinkled the skin at the corners of his eyes. "As a matter of fact, I don't. That was from Don."

"Huh?"

"He said he owed you one from New Year's Eve two years ago and made me promise to deliver it."

She stared up at him in total incomprehension. Logan hooked a brow and attempted to prompt a nonexistent memory.

"He abandoned you at the Waldorf. Five minutes before midnight. To deliver twins."

"I don't have a clue who or what you're…"

Understanding burst like a water balloon.

"Wait a sec. Are you talking about Sabrina's old boyfriend? Your buddy, who's now an ob-gyn doc?"

It was Logan's turn to look startled. He recovered

faster than Devon had, though. His smile widened into a rueful grin.

"I take it you're not Sabrina Russo."

"No, Mr. Logan, I am *not*."

* * * * *

Be sure to look for
THE CEO'S CHRISTMAS PROPOSITION
by Merline Lovelace.
Available in November 2008 wherever books are sold,
including most bookstores, supermarkets, drugstores
and discount stores.

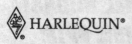
HARLEQUIN®

American ★ Romance®

LAURA MARIE ALTOM
A Daddy
for Christmas

THE STATE OF PARENTHOOD

Single mom Jesse Cummings is struggling
to run her Oklahoma ranch and raise her
two little girls after the death of her husband.
Then on Christmas Eve, a miracle strolls onto
her land in the form of tall, handsome bull
rider Gage Moore. He doesn't plan on staying,
but in the season of miracles, anything
can happen....

**Available November
wherever books are sold.**

LOVE, HOME & HAPPINESS

REQUEST YOUR FREE BOOKS!
2 FREE NOVELS PLUS 2 FREE GIFTS!

HARLEQUIN®

Super Romance®

Exciting, emotional, unexpected!

YES! Please send me 2 FREE Harlequin Superromance® novels and my 2 FREE gifts (gifts are worth about $10). After receiving them, if I don't wish to receive any more books, I can return the shipping statement marked "cancel." If I don't cancel, I will receive 6 brand-new novels every month and be billed just $4.69 per book in the U.S. or $5.24 per book in Canada, plus 25¢ shipping and handling per book and applicable taxes, if any*. That's a savings of close to 15% off the cover price! I understand that accepting the 2 free books and gifts places me under no obligation to buy anything. I can always return a shipment and cancel at any time. Even if I never buy another book from Harlequin, the two free books and gifts are mine to keep forever.

135 HDN EEX7 336 HDN EEYK

Name	(PLEASE PRINT)	
Address		Apt. #
City	State/Prov.	Zip/Postal Code

Signature (if under 18, a parent or guardian must sign)

Mail to the Harlequin Reader Service:
IN U.S.A.: P.O. Box 1867, Buffalo, NY 14240-1867
IN CANADA: P.O. Box 609, Fort Erie, Ontario L2A 5X3

Not valid to current subscribers of Harlequin Superromance books.

Want to try two free books from another line?
Call 1-800-873-8635 or visit www.morefreebooks.com.

* Terms and prices subject to change without notice. N.Y. residents add applicable sales tax. Canadian residents will be charged applicable provincial taxes and GST. Offer not valid in Quebec. This offer is limited to one order per household. All orders subject to approval. Credit or debit balances in a customer's account(s) may be offset by any other outstanding balance owed by or to the customer. Please allow 4 to 6 weeks for delivery. Offer available while quantities last.

Your Privacy: Harlequin is committed to protecting your privacy. Our Privacy Policy is available online at www.eHarlequin.com or upon request from the Reader Service. From time to time we make our lists of customers available to reputable third parties who may have a product or service of interest to you. If you would prefer we not share your name and address, please check here. ☐

HSR08R

Romantic
SUSPENSE

Sparked by Danger, Fueled by Passion.

Lindsay McKenna
Susan Grant

Mission: Christmas

Celebrate the holidays with a pair
of military heroines and their daring men
in two romantic, adventurous stories
from these bestselling authors.

Featuring:

"The Christmas Wild Bunch"
by *USA TODAY* bestselling author
Lindsay McKenna

and

"Snowbound with a Prince"
by *New York Times* bestselling author
Susan Grant

Available November wherever books are sold.

HARLEQUIN *Super Romance*

COMING NEXT MONTH

HSRCNMBPA1008